His ideas a[...]
were entirely wrong

"Why did you do it?" Sara demanded, her voice husky with emotion.

"You mean why did I follow you upstairs to your room? Because I wanted to, that's why," John answered. "A man would have to be blind not to want—"

"I don't make a practice of entertaining men in my bedroom!"

"Look," he snapped, "you went out with my brother. You did come back with all your clothes on, so I do give you some credit."

"Poor John," she half whispered. "I really didn't enjoy it, you know."

He stared at her; a whole host of emotions fleeting across his face. "I don't need your pity, Sara. That's the last thing I want!"

WELCOME
TO THE WONDERFUL WORLD
OF *Harlequin Presents*

Interesting, informative and entertaining,
each Harlequin Presents portrays an appealing
and original love story. With a varied array
of settings, we may lure you on an African safari,
to a quaint Welsh village, or an exotic Riviera
location—anywhere and everywhere that adventurous
men and women fall in love.

As publishers of Harlequin Presents, we're
extremely proud of our books. Since 1949,
Harlequin Enterprises has built its publishing
reputation on the solid base of quality and
originality. Our stories are the most popular
paperback romances sold in North America; every
month, eight new titles are released and sold at
nearly every book-selling store in Canada and the
United States.

A free catalog listing all Harlequin Presents
can be yours by writing to the

HARLEQUIN READER SERVICE,
(In the U.S.) P.O. Box 52040, Phoenix, AZ 85072-2040
(In Canada) Stratford, Ontario, N5A 6W2

We sincerely hope you enjoy reading
this Harlequin Presents.

Yours truly,

THE PUBLISHERS
Harlequin Presents

EMMA GOLDRICK

and blow your house down

Harlequin Books

TORONTO • NEW YORK • LONDON
AMSTERDAM • PARIS • SYDNEY • HAMBURG
STOCKHOLM • ATHENS • TOKYO • MILAN

Harlequin Presents first edition May 1984
ISBN 0-373-10688-2

Original hardcover edition published in 1983
by Mills & Boon Limited

CHAPTER ONE

THE cold east wind whistled as it wandered over the grey May-tinted waters of Buzzards Bay and then out into the white-capped Atlantic. Sara shivered as she squatted on the sand just above the high water mark. The whole expanse of beach which outlined Point Judith was unmarked, save for her own footprints. Warily she scanned the sand on all sides of her. To her right the open door of her cottage offered haven from the wind. Straight ahead, about two hundred yards away, were the rotten timbers of Burton's Wharf. Half blinded, she scoured the inches of sand with both eye and hand. When the shadow came between her and the setting sun she stopped, and turned her head slowly to the right. The toe of a large black shoe, highly polished, rested in the sand at her side.

Slowly she shifted her weight backwards to avoid moving her feet, then she wrapped her hands around her legs just below the knees to maintain her balance. She looked up. The sun was in her eyes, and her left eye could not focus. She could barely discern the outline of a man, dressed in a dark pinstripe suit.

'You're too big,' she said softly in her deep husky voice. 'You're blocking the light!'

He laughed and squatted down at her side. 'Not too big,' he said. 'Barely six feet. It seems big because you're so little.'

'Short,' she replied coldly. 'Short!'

'Hmm?'

'I am not little—I am short.'

'And sensitive about it, huh? What are you? Fifteen? You have plenty of time to get your growth. I wanted to ask you——'

'Don't count on it. I've got my growth. I'm older than you think.'

5

'Yes, well, I'm sure you are. I wanted to ask you if——'

'Please, don't move your feet,' she pleaded. 'I've lost one of my contact lenses. It just slipped out, but I can't see without my glasses and——'

'Hold tight,' he returned. His voice was deep and vibrant, and as he leaned closer she could see a craggy, lined face, wide between the eyes. Craggy, but not unhandsome, she thought. Black hair, short and wavy, not responsive to discipline. Dark eyes. She closed her left eye and managed to get a clear look through her right. Dark brown eyes—bold commanding eyes. Thick eyelashes that met each other just over an aquiline nose. A broad smile, and flashing white teeth!

For some reason she felt conscious of the clothes she was wearing. The well-worn sneakers were ideal for the beach, but her denims had long since lost their deep blue, and with Uncle Harry's sweatshirt pulled on over her own cardigan she looked a shapeless sack. The torn ends of the sweatshirt fell to her thighs and flapped in the wind. She shrugged her two straw-coloured pigtails back over her shoulders and waited.

'I don't mean to be rude, my dear,' he said, 'but I've travelled a long way today to find someone, and I'm rather tired. Ah—there! There's a shiny spot in the sand just by your left toe. Try that.' He hunkered back on his heels in the manner of an accomplished athlete who had stretched his tendons early in life.

Sara reached down carefully, tracing the sand with her fingertips until they touched a smooth surface. She fingered the lens and held it up before her right eye for examination.

'That's it!' She unfolded herself upwards without using her hands. He did the same, and she was startled at the grace of his movement.

'Perhaps you really ought to wear glasses,' he suggested. There was a tinge of solemnity and remoteness in his tone. She had heard it many times before. A 'let's be nice to the little girl' tone. She giggled.

'I have glasses in the cottage,' she said softly, 'but they're bad for business. I'm trying to get accustomed to these lenses before I go back to work.'

'Work?' he snorted. 'A kid like you? How come you're not in school?'

'Who are you, the truant officer?' she demanded.

'No, damn it, just a man looking for a woman!'

'You should go into town for that. There's not much call for that sort of thing out here.'

'Don't be impertinent, kid. I'm looking for a particular woman who supposedly lives in this area. And while we're at it, you need to be a little more careful. A girl out here on the beach alone! Anything could happen to you, you know. How come you're not in school?'

'I left school some time ago.' Sara couldn't restrain the smile that lit up her wind-red face. 'I'm older than you think. Besides, I'm not alone. Mary is always with me.'

'You may have dropped out of school, but I'll bet a bundle you're barely sixteen. Who's Mary? I don't see her anywhere.'

'Well, she sees you. She's up there on the porch.'

He reached out towards her, putting a hand on each of her shoulders and turning her into the sun. 'Let me look at you——' he started to say.

'I wouldn't do that if I were you,' she said quickly. 'Mary won't like that. You'd better take your hands off me, Mr—oh lordy, it's too late! Don't run—please don't run! Stand very still!'

She dropped to the sand, away from his hands, then scrambled a couple of steps up the slope of the beach. 'It's okay, Mary!' she yelled. 'Stop, Mary!'

He turned as he heard the scrabbling of claws on wood, but before he could take a step the sound resolved itself into the racing black hulk of a huge Labrador retriever. The dog hurled at him, throwing itself through the air for the last four feet, smashing into him just above the knees. He dropped in a sprawled mass on to the sand, and the dog stood over him, stiff-legged, drooling jaws just inches from his throat.

'Please, Mr——' Sara began.

'Englewood,' he gasped. 'John Englewood. Get this wolf off of me!' The dog growled and inched closer.

'Please, Mr Englewood,' Sara pleaded, 'please don't move. And don't make any more smart remarks—Mary is sensitive about that kind of talk. She's not a wolf. Please don't make a move—not even a finger.'

'John,' he muttered through clenched teeth. 'Call me——'

'Oh, shut up,' she retorted. 'Just shut up!' Softly, gently, she dropped to her knees and began to croon to the dog, an endless repetition of soothing sounds. 'Sara loves Mary,' she hummed, 'Mary loves Sara.' Slowly she caressed the rough black stubble of fur, then she wrapped her arms around the dog's neck. 'Sara loves Mary,' she monotoned in the dog's ear. 'Mary loves Sara!'

Gradually the stiff forelegs of the huge dog relaxed, and it began to pant. Sara increased her weight on the dog's neck, hugging it closely. 'Mary,' she commanded, 'sit!' And then a little louder, a little more forcefully, 'Mary—sit!' The big dog hesitated, turned its massive head away from the man still sprawled frozen in the sand, and then, with a grunt, sank on to its haunches.

'Thank God!' John Englewood, who had been holding his breath, began to inhale again. The dog turned back towards him, and half rose. Sara continued to stroke the dog while she talked to the man. 'Watch yourself now. Don't make a move. I have to convince Mary that we're really friends.'

Still crooning to the dog, Sara unwound her arms from around the animal. Then she slowly crawled on hands and knees until she knelt by the man's head. 'Don't move!' she whispered. Then she leaned over and gently brushed her lips across his cheek. The dog whined. Once more she leaned down and gently pressed her soft lips against his, in the merest brush of contact. Out of the corner of her eye she saw the big dog relax, and heard the thump as Mary stretched out on the sand. As she straightened up she smiled down at John Englewood. 'See?' she chuckled.

But somehow he wasn't laughing. Those tremendous arms reached up and enfolded her, gently pulling her back down to him. His lips caressed hers, like a fleeting gust of wind. Then they returned, pressing harder against the softness of her mouth. She was startled by her own response. For some reason she found the pressure, the exploring lips that probed at the inner slope of her mouth, she found it all very—pleasant. And when finally the steel bands released her she fell backwards on to her heels, struggling to catch a breath, bemused by it all, her cheeks flushed a brilliant red.

'See?' he chuckled in that deep clear voice that seemed to make her tiny frame vibrate. 'Do we do it again, or could I get up now?'

Sara was still struggling to get her breath back under control. 'Mary?' she called. But the big dog was evidently satisfied, and was already half way back to the warmth and dryness of the porch. For some reason Sara felt bereft, as if her best friend had just taken her to the low-tide mark and thrown her into the ocean. She put her hands on her hips and muttered, 'And that's gratitude for you, you big fake!'

She turned back to the man, closing her left eye to bring him in focus. He was still on the sand, staring at her, examining every detail of her with those deep dark eyes. She unfolded herself, brushing the sand from her denims, examining him as he did her.

'I'm really very sorry,' she gasped, reaching out a hand to help him. 'You understand that we—that she's really not like this all the time. It's just that she's a trained guard dog, you know—she's not a pet. And it's just been a terrible day so far, and I didn't get nearly enough clams to make supper, and Mary worries about me, and—and I do believe we've torn your trousers and made a mess of your fine suit. I *am* sorry. You will accept my apology, please? Mary never apologises, and——' By that time her mind had caught up to her mouth. She stifled her babbling by the simple expedient of sticking her fist in her mouth.

He laughed as he tried to brush sand from his suit coat. 'I don't need Mary's apology,' he replied. 'All I need to know is that she isn't going to bite me!'

'Oh no,' she assured him, trying to help with the brushing-off. 'She never attacks a kissing friend. And she doesn't have the killer instinct. She's a drop-out from the Army Guard Dog programme. But of course you shouldn't have put your hands on me, you know.' Her hand had been brushing the side of his jacket and his larger, heavier fingers brushed across hers. Her voice rose to a squeak and then trailed away as she blushed again. She turned her back to him and concentrated on the low hills of Scraggy Neck, just across the bay.

When she finally managed to regain control of her wandering nerves she turned back to him. She clasped her hands behind her and looked up at him. 'Why don't you come up to the cottage, Mr Englewood? Perhaps we can do something to repair——'

'John,' he interrupted. 'My name is John. Mr Englewood was my father. Sweet sixteen and never been kissed, Sara?'

'Yes,' she mumbled. 'I mean—no. And yes.'

'Which answer for which question?'

'No, I'm not sweet sixteen. No, I've been kissed before. Yes, my name is Sara. Does that satisfy you?'

'The question is, does it satisfy you, Sara?'

'I—er—I don't know what you mean.'

'You know, Sara. You know,' he drawled.

She shrugged her shoulders to break herself out of the hypnotic moment. 'The little basket,' she said. 'That's all the clams I've dug. Bring it, please.' He moved up the beach, swinging her straw basket up with a single finger. She held back momentarily, looking at the grey sea, the bright sun, the gleaming white underbellies of the seagulls diving just offshore. Why does it all look so different now? she wondered. So much brighter, so much more comforting?

The cottage had been a simple weatherbeaten Cape Codder, designed for summer living, but now fully insulated for year-round occupation. Only the tiny flower bed filled with a riot of late blooming jonquils, peonies, crocuses and azaleas, set it apart from the other thirty cottages that dotted the Point. They climbed the four steps to the porch and went through the open door. Most of the first floor was a combined living-dining room. The furniture was sparse, but well polished. An enormous handmade braided rug covered the centre of the floor. A small dining table took up the far end of the room, against the two back windows. Three doors led off to the right, all opened. The first was a small bedroom, the second a tiny white-tiled bathroom, and the third an equally tiny kitchen. A narrow flight of stairs, almost a ladder, led to the sleeping loft above.

'Your family lives here?' John Englewood asked as she helped him off with his coat. 'Damn! I've got sand down my neck and in my shoes.'

'No,' she replied, 'I live here by myself—me and Mary. Sometimes Uncle Harry comes. Why don't you get out of all those things and get a shower?' she added. 'You could wear Uncle Harry's robe while I brush all this sand off your clothes. And would you stay for supper?'

He laughed down at her, and the pleasure-crinkles around his mouth transformed his face completely. 'I would really like to, Sara, but my time is very limited. I've got six harebrained graduate students who still haven't had their thesis subject approved. And we're having trouble with both the apple and the tobacco crop. And on top of all that my brother Robert told me this morning that there'll surely be a strike at the family manufacturing plant. So with all that on my plate, then came this crazy clause in Aunt Lucinda's will, and I have to hare off on a wild goose chase after some stupid woman who evidently caught my aunt's eye.'

'You've got more troubles than me!' Sara chuckled. 'So what are you, Mr—er—John? A farmer? A corporation owner? What else?'

'In descending order of interest, Sara, I'm an Assistant Professor of Engineering at the University of Massachusetts. And then I own a farm. And then I share with the family in a small electronics plant. But right now I'm playing Sherlock Holmes. My Aunt Lucinda—Lucinda Craven—owned the large summer house behind your cottage. Perhaps you'd met her?'

Sara ducked her head to hide her confusion. As he talked she had been unbraiding her hair to shake the sand and salt out of it. She used it now to cover her expression, and contributed a 'hmm' to the conversation. John hardly seemed to have noticed.

'Well, Aunt Lucinda died a month ago, and her will is creating all kinds of little problems. She knew a woman around here someplace, by the name of Susan Antonia Rebecca Anderson. You could hardly miss with a name like that, could you? Do you know where I might find her?'

Sara bustled around, collecting his coat, tie, and shoes.

'I guess I've heard the name,' she replied softly. 'Why don't you get your shower and then we could talk about it at supper?'

'Must be some kind of a charmer, Sara. Older than you, of course. And she must live in this area—well, at least within walking distance.'

'After your shower.' She pushed him towards the bathroom door. After he had disappeared she wiggled out of Uncle Harry's sweatshirt and dashed up the stairs to where her uncle's fishing clothes hung on an open rack. She made a quick selection of robe and running pants, then walked slowly down the stairs. She stopped long enough to remove her single contact lens, drop the pair into cleaning fluid, and don her hornrimmed glasses. Then she pulled out a chair and sat down. Mary wandered in from the porch, huffing as if she had just finished the Boston Marathon. Sara reached down and idly scratched the tiny bald spot on the top of the dog's head.

'What in the world do you make of it, Mary?' she whispered. 'He knows my whole name! And Aunt Cindy left a will? What in the world——?' Mary huffed a couple of times and looked up, waiting. 'And he's such a big man, Mary. Ain't it wonderful? I haven't really seen a big man since the boys moved away and Papa died! But what a strange one. A college professor, a farmer—and he wears pinstriped suits. A little pompous? What could he want of me? And listen—he sings a passable Lord High Executioner, doesn't he? Or maybe it's just the shower that turns him on. David was like that. But keep your eyes open, Mary, until we find out what he really wants!'

Mary managed to present a fairly passable 'Whuff!'

'That too,' Sara laughed. She strolled over and knocked on the door, interrupting a terrible basso profundo attempt to sing Nanki-Poo. 'A robe and some pants,' she shouted over the roar to the shower. She threw the clothes in, rescued his trousers, closed the door behind her, and rested against its frame. The water continued to splash in the shower. Sara closed her eyes and tried to imagine the lanky length of him under the errant hot-water shower. She pulled off both her sweaters and tossed them on the sofa. Her own white T-shirt revealed the full swelling of her mature figure. 'America's Cup rigging on a ten-foot hull,' Grandfather used to say. Thoughtfully she ran her hands down her sides, from breast to thigh, daydreaming that they just might be—his hands. The water in the shower stopped, and the sudden quiet shocked her into recognising just what it was she had been thinking.

The blush started at her throat and raced across her face until even the tips of her ears had turned red. She ran up the stairs, taking them two at a time, and slid into the anonymity of one of her brother Ralph's old flannel shirts.

When John came out of the shower he looked scrubbed and brushed, and not at all out of place in Uncle Harry's robe. Sara waved him to a seat, and took his suit out to hang on the line behind the cottage. She frowned at the gash in the knee of his trousers, and brought them back in with her.

'There are drinks in the refrigerator,' she offered. 'I don't keep any hard liquor here, but there are a few cans of beer. I'll try to stitch up this tear in your trousers.'

He ambled out to the kitchen as she assumed the yoga-position on the sofa and reached into her sewing box. When he returned with two beers she was already at work, taking tiny stitches on the reverse side of the trouser-leg, leaning over her work with her frame glasses balanced precariously on the end of her upturned nose. She waved away his offering.

'I never drink anything alcoholic,' she murmured as she bit the thread. John settled himself into a chair opposite her, and sucked at his own can.

'Homey atmosphere, Sara,' he commented, saluting her with the raised beer can. 'You cook, you sew, you keep a house, and you work. Are there any more at home like you? You aren't married, are you?'

'Me?' she squeaked. 'Of course not! I'm a bachelor working girl.'

'You mean a spinster?'

She glared at him, but refused to be baited.

'Where does your family live? Somewhere around here?' he asked.

'No. My mother and father are both dead, and the boys have scattered all around the country. And you?'

'No, I'm not married either. Not now. My wife died about three years ago. I have a seven-year-old son, and a brother, and we all live in the western part of Massachusetts, near the town of South Deerfield. You know the area?'

'Nope.' She handed him his trousers. 'I'm afraid that's the best I can do. Sewing's not my line of work. Mother tried to make a 'compleat domestic' out of me, but I—well, maybe it will get you home.'

'Looks fine to me,' he commented. 'Now, what can you tell me about Susan Anderson?'

'You said she was older than me?' She tried to freeze a bland placid expression on her face, but without much success.

'I don't really know, but I have to assume from what my aunt wrote that the woman is quite mature.'

'Your aunt wrote about m—Susan in her will?'

'Yes. A ridiculous provision, but it's holding up the probate of the entire will, and my brother Robert is concerned. Did you know my aunt?'

'Yes, I knew her. We called her Aunt Cindy. I— we heard she'd died. I would have come to the funeral, but my mother died that same week, and——' Sara jumped up from the sofa and made off towards the kitchen as fast as she could move, turning her head away from him to hide the tears.

'Now what are you running from?' he called. 'What are you up to now?'

'I have to start the supper,' she replied, avoiding a direct confrontation with him. 'I didn't get enough clams today, but the night before last we had steamed clams, and I saved the juice. Do you like clam chowder?'

'Yes. New England style, of course. I can't stand that New York stuff.'

'Can you peel potatoes?' she asked. 'The paring knife is in the little drawer there.' She busied herself setting the pan of clam juice on the butane burner, and fumbling for onions and seasoning.

'As easy as that?' he asked.

'Of course. The water left over from the steaming has the flavour of the clams. We just add onions, diced potatoes, and a little flavouring. Then we'll shuck these few clams I got today, and add them to the pile. When the potatoes are finished, we add milk, simmer it all, and there we are.'

'It *is* easy, isn't it,' John commented. Then his hands touched her shoulders and turned her away from the stove. 'Now just tell me, Sara, why it is that every time we start to have a sensible conversation the subject gets changed? Susan Anderson—do you know her?'

'You're not peeling the potatoes very efficiently. You're cutting the——'

'For the love of heaven, Sara, just answer the question! Susan Anderson. Do you know who she is?'

'If she was older than me it could have been my aunt. Aunt Susan.'

John glared as she picked up a sharp knife and began shucking the clams. Then she tried to appear intensely busy as she dropped the clams into a wire strainer to rinse off the sand. After a moment of this he turned her around again, and held her chin up between his strong fingers. 'Susan Anderson. Perhaps you could tell me how to get in touch with your Aunt Susan?' His voice had gone silky-soft, and somewhat threatening.

'I don't think so,' she muttered, and turned so red that he could see the flush spreading up into her hairline. 'She died about six years ago.'

'All right, Sara, come to the point. Susan Antonia Rebecca Anderson?' He said the names slowly, with heavy accent on the first letter of each name. 'Susan Antonia Rebecca Anderson! Sara?'

'Yes,' she sighed. She shrugged her shoulders, edged over to the kitchen stool and sat down. 'I have to tell you the whole story,' she said, 'or you won't understand at all.'

'I'm waiting.'

'My dad was a big man, over six foot three. All my brothers except David are six foot two. David is six foot seven. He——'

'A basketball player?'

'Who, David? No, he lives in Dallas, Texas. Well, anyway, my mother was tall for a woman, five foot ten. And then there's me.'

'Five foot nothing, Sara? Sara for short?'

She drew herself up to the height of her small dignity. 'Five foot and three quarters,' she proclaimed. 'I wear heels a lot. Well, I was premature, you know. They thought I wouldn't live past the first day, so they christened me with all the names of my aunts who had no children of their own. But of course I fooled them. When I got to be seven years old I was a midget in a family of giants, and David—he's my youngest brother—decided that my name was too long for such a short person, and so he decided to call me——'

'Of course—Sara for short. Did it make you angry?'

'For a little while. I was becoming very selfconscious about it, until Mamma asked me to conduct an experiment. Put those potatoes in the water now, please.'

'What was the experiment?'

'They were all so big, you know, that when I wanted to kiss one of them I had to climb up on a chair to reach. Well, I just caught each one of them alone, and I smiled at them, and told them that I wanted to kiss them, and I stood very still.'

'And then?'

'I found that I didn't need a chair. They all bent over so that I could reach them. It was a very satisfactory thing for a short person to realise she had that much power over tall people, believe me!'

"Ah! your mother was a psychologist?"

'No, she was a surgeon.'

'And that's how you became "Sara for Short"?'

'Yes—a family joke with a double meaning. And it's nice for a girl to have three big brothers, let me tell you. Your Aunt Cindy met them all at our reunion party four years ago.'

'Aunt Cindy,' he laughed. 'She would have killed us if we ever called her that! But why would a cold fish like Aunt Lucinda put you in her will?'

'She was no cold fish!' Sara raged. 'She was a lonely old lady, and full of fun. Did you ever come down here with her? I must say that if her family had loved her, perhaps——'

Her solemn lecture was cut off in midstream by a chortle of laughter from the bedroom. Sara quickly dumped the rest of the onions and seasonings into the boiling kettle, then wiped her hands on her apron. She looked up at John. He was staring at her with a cold look in his eyes. His lips were pressed harshly together. 'A child?' he asked arrogantly.

'Of course,' she retorted.

She walked out into the living room just in time to see her little nephew wobble around the corner of the bedroom door and plop himself down on the living-room floor. Sara stood still, but stretched out her hands to him, aware that the man beside her was searching her face.

'Come on, Pudge,' she coaxed. The little boy turned over on his stomach, levered himself back on his feet, and wobbled towards her. A big grin split his chubby fourteen-month-old face. When he reached Sara's questing fingers she swung him up into her arms and cuddled him against her face, at which point he destroyed the serenity of the moment by roaring the only word in his vocabulary. 'Momma,' he roared, immensely pleased with himself. 'Momma!'

She jiggled his twenty-eight pounds on to her hip and tickled his ribs. He responded with a wiggle and another roar of laughter. She carried him over to the dining table and stretched him out.

'Here, let me do that,' the deep voice at her shoulder said. Sara looked back at him, startled. A small smile played at the corners of his heavy lips. 'An old hand,' said John, edging her aside. 'Done it for years.' And without a qualm he stripped Pudge of his shorts, discarded the wet nappy, powdered and patted his bottom, added a new disposable nappy, and set the baby back down on the floor.

'He looks like a miniature edition of yourself,' he said.

'Of course he does,' she replied. 'We're very closely related.' She picked up the wet nappy and carried it into the kitchen.

'Very closely. Of course.' It was a statement he was making, rather than a question. Sara looked up at his stern face and wondered at the frown that chased across his rugged features.

'Tell me something about you and Aunt—Cindy,' he asked.

She smiled at him, pleased at the pleasant memories. Pudge was playing with Mary's tail and was fully occupied. 'Aunt Cindy,' she mused, stirring the chowder with her wooden spoon. 'Regular as clockwork. Came down in June, and left on Labor Day. She visited with me most days. We walked on the beach and went out in my boat a few times, but it sank, you know—the boat did. Can you find the black pepper?

'And then we all used to sit on the porch of an evening, me and Mamma and your aunt. She was such a lonely person. She just wanted to talk about her home in the Valley, and about her nephews, and—oh, you know, woman-talk. I enjoyed it. I worked nights mostly then, and it was nice to have a reasonable gam before going off on one of my cases.'

'One of your cases?'

'Well, you know—I used to work in Boston. But that got awful tiresome—same place, same time, same faces. And then my mother became ill, so I came down to New Bedford. We have an arrangement, you know, about twenty of us girls. Mendonca—she retired some years ago—she keeps a list of all of us available to work, and people call her. And then she gets in touch with us, and off we go.'

'All this investment just for one night?'

'You've got it all mixed up,' she laughed, aware again that he was studying her face. 'We don't do one-night stands. Sometimes it's a week, sometimes two. I prefer the older people, myself. They're more demanding, but more fun.'

'So then you go off and spend a week or two. And then what?'

'I always like to take a little break between cases. It pays very well, you know.'

'I'm afraid I don't know, Sara. But I'm getting an

inkling about what Aunt Lucinda wanted.'

Sara didn't understand, but refused to be caught up in another round of debate with him. 'Watch the baby,' she commanded, and began to set the table.

After dinner John helped her clear the table, then went with her as she stripped the baby and dumped him in the tub. 'Let me do that,' he suggested. He rolled up the sleeves of the robe, knelt down by the enamelled tub, and spent a pleasant fifteen minutes washing and teasing Pudge. The baby enjoyed it all, and proceeded to blow a few bubbles for his entertainment.

Sara rocked back on her heels and watched these two males amuse each other. When Pudge grows up they'll be much alike, she thought. He's nice when he isn't being so pompous. But I suppose university professors get that way. But what in the world could Aunt Cindy have meant by putting her in the will? Look at the size of his shoulders! Wouldn't David approve of him in a hurry? But such a—crinkly face. Nobody would call him handsome—but then—He looks like Abraham Lincoln!

He had spoken twice before she heard. 'We're both waterlogged, Sara. Grab this little rascal!' He was laughing, and Pudge was chortling. Water dripped from both their faces. Guiltily Sara snatched up a mammoth bath towel, completely wrapped her nephew in it, from head to toe, and carried him out to the sofa to play their usual game.

'What have I got in this package?' she called out. 'Where has Pudge disappeared to? Well, I can't find him. I think I'll drop this package on the floor and go look for Pudge.' With which she dropped the baby two feet on to the sofa, where he bounced, poked his head out from the towel, and laughed hugely. She began to give him a gentle rub-down.

'Your suit ought to be blown clean, Mr—John,' she said. 'Why don't you finish towelling the little rascal while I bring it in, then you can get dressed. By that time Pudge will be ready for bed again, and we can talk.'

Despite her assurances it was almost an hour before Pudge was settled down with a bottle of warm milk to soothe him.

'Where are you spending the night?' she asked John.

'I really had no plan. Is there a motel or a hotel anywhere in the area?'

'Nothing closer than New Bedford—that's about seventeen miles. And most of the motels haven't opened yet. We don't get the tourists for another month. Would you like to stay here? I could move Pudge out of Uncle Harry's bedroom, and you could use that?'

'That would be convenient, but hardly proper. What would the neighbours think?'

'Don't be silly! I sleep up in the loft, and Mary sleeps at the foot of the stairs. Everybody knows that. Besides, one scream out of me and half the male population of the Point would be at the door!'

'They all like you so much?'

'Why, of course. They all know me. I'm a sort of one-of-a-kind person around these parts.'

After a little debate he agreed, and helped her to move Pudge's playpen into the darkened kitchen. After the baby had settled, the two of them sat down at the table again, and nursed mugs of coffee. The sun had already dropped below the horizon, and the soft twilight had stilled the raucous hawking of the gulls for the first time that day. They watched from the window as the gathering darkness absorbed the grey-white caps of the waves colliding at Colters Rip.

'About my aunt,' John said at last.

'She was a sweet and kind woman. We all knew she had cancer. I'm very sorry she died, John. And I'm happy that she left me some little remembrance.'

'It's not hardly a little remembrance,' he commented. His voice had lost its previous warmth, and his eyes seemed to have deepened, become unreadable pools. Sara could not control the quiver that ran up her spine. She sat stiffly in her chair, both hands in her lap, her fingers twisting and turning as they usually did when she was uncomfortable.

'I have to tell you something about the Englewoods,' he began. 'Mind if I smoke?'

'I do mind,' she said softly. 'Smoking upsets me.'

He had already drawn a pack of cigarettes from his pocket, and was caught halfway towards lighting up. Her refusal startled him so much that he stopped in mid-motion, then carefully restored the cigarette to the pack and the pack to his pocket. 'I'm sorry——' he started to say, but she waved him aside.

'Go on about your aunt,' she asked.

'Our family—the Englewoods. We own a manufacturing plant in South Deerfield. Practically all the shares of stock are owned by the family. I hold forty-one per cent, my brother Robert owns forty per cent, Aunt Lucinda had fifteen per cent, and the remainder are owned by some of our senior employees, and the Union. You follow me?' Sara nodded her head and tried not to appear ignorant. Uncle Harry, who had been a stockbroker on the New York Exchange for forty years, had been very discouraged when Sara chose nursing as a career, rather than to accept his invitation to join his firm.

'So here's the problem. Aunt Lucinda has left her shares of stock in a trust. They represent an important and essential part of our management control, you understand. The trust runs for three years. If, during that three years, I'm able to comply with the second requirement of her will, those shares will revert to me.'

'Giving you absolute control of the company? What's the second requirement?'

'The absolute control isn't important. Robert and I have absolute control already. We're very close. We never never disagree—at least, we never do about the company policy!'

'So what was the second requirement?'

John was embarrassed. He ran a finger around the collar of his shirt, and leaned forward into the light of the lamp which Sara had just ignited. 'The second requirement, Sara, is that some time during those three years I must persuade Susan Anderson to come and live in my house for a six-month period!'

She gulped the too-hot coffee in complete surprise, and was startled again when the overheated liquid slid down her throat, half choking her. It took a few minutes to recover her control.

'Why in the world?' she gasped. 'Why in the world would she make such a provision as that? I certainly wouldn't consider—what happens if I don't come?'

'Two things, Sara. First for the period of the trust, whether you come or not, you receive all income from this block of stock, and have the voting rights they entail. Then, at the end of three years, should you not come, the entire estate reverts to the absolute ownership of—Susan Anderson.'

'Oh, my!' she stuttered. 'Let me understand you. If I come, you get the stock. And if I don't come, *I* get the stock. Isn't that a peculiar arrangement? What could she have been thinking of?' she mused. Certainly not just to give Sara a home and an income. No one knew better than Aunt Cindy how well off her parents had left her at their death, and how pleased Sara was with her career. Why would—and then she recalled a scene from the previous autumn. Summer had come to a chilly end, but Aunt Cindy had lingered longer at the sea-coast than she usually did. The two of them had been sitting on the porch steps, watching the gulls drop shellfish on the rocks to crack them open. The pallor of cancer was already on the older woman's face, and they both knew that this would be their last summer together.

'You know, Sara,' Aunt Cindy has said, 'you've made such a wonderful change in my life these last five years. They've been the happiest I've ever known. Some day I shall ask you to do an even greater job—straightening out the terrible mess my family is in.'

'Of course!' Sara exclaimed. 'It's got nothing at all to do with the shares!' The troubled man sitting across from her looked up.

'What?' he asked. 'What who meant? What are you talking about now?'

'Nothing. Nothing at all,' Sara sighed. She sat silently, staring at nothing. Then she looked back at him. 'It still sounds pretty silly, John. What would either of us gain?'

'The advantages are all on my side, Sara. If you comply, I get all the shares. They're worth roughly two hundred thousand dollars. On the other hand, you get an income from them for three years—that could amount to almost ten thousand a year. You also get an all-expenses-paid vacation in the Connecticut Valley, and with it a chance to get away from all this—this work that you do.'

'But that doesn't signify, John. I love my work. And what good is a six-month vacation? It would drive me up the wall!'

'I know the shares are a tremendous attraction, Sara, but I'm convinced that the vacation will do you some good. The shares are not all that important to me. Think about it.'

'They're not all that important to me either,' she confessed. But then she began to give it the thought that he had recommended. Go with him? Why not? For two months she had been a beachcomber, washing out of her mind the sorrow of her mother's slow death, and the attendant pain of knowing that all her nursing skills could do nothing to keep death at bay. And now, stirring within her, was the need to grasp life again, to be about and doing. Aunt Cindy had left her a puzzle to be solved, a puzzle that obviously had nothing to do with money or stocks or control of corporations. Was that what she was meant to do? Solve the puzzle? Or were there deeper troubles, darker concerns to which she might turn her skills? There could be nothing to fear. Mary would go with her, and if she could not find the answers, she could turn back to the sea-coast and all her friends on the Point. But as she tried to reason this all out logically, John's face kept flashing in and out of focus in her mind, and suddenly she knew a startling truth. He was the piper who drew her uncontrollably; she would go with him because he asked her to, and nothing else really mattered!

She was just about to tell him of her decision when the hail came from the front porch.

'Hello, Sara. You're ready for us?'

Mary snapped to attention and growled. John looked a question at Sara.

'Henry Gomez,' she answered his unspoken query. 'I forgot—I promised him something. Would you mind——' He waved his acquiescence, and she walked over to the door and opened it.

'So, Mr Gomez, I almost forgot. Come in, please. And this is George? Come in and sit down, Mr Gomez.'

The man who came in was short, barely five foot six, but as wide as two ordinary men. He seethed with muscles, his arms looked like tree-logs, his face was wrinkled and burned by much exposure to sea winds. He looked the perfect example of a mature Portuguese fisherman. His lanky son, who followed him in, was taller, much thinner, with a pimpled face and obviously shy in present company. Sara made the introductions.

'You promise, Sara, hey?' the man said. 'Tomorrow the boy becomes fifteen, he is a man. And you promise to break him in, no?'

'Yes, I promised, Mr Gomez,' Sara laughed. 'This sort of thing is always difficult. Why don't you sit here on the couch and talk with Mr Englewood? This won't take long. Into the bedroom, George.' She followed the young man into the tiny room and shut the door.

There was a moment of uneasy silence in the living room after they had left.

'Your son?' asked John Englewood diffidently.

'Yes—my only son. And this is an important time, no? Sara has say she will do this thing. Nobody better than Sara, I tell you, Mr Englewood. You don't come from around here?'

'No, I don't, Mr Gomez. I come from the other end of Massachusetts. Sara is good at this, you say?'

'The best. Special good she is with the young ones. Let me tell you something, that girl is the top of the pile, no? I could take him in the city, you understand, but nobody is better than Sara!'

John Englewood looked very uncomfortable, and rather than continue the conversation he picked up a copy of the *National Geographic* from the book-rack beside his chair and imitated a studious reader. Henry Gomez watched him for a few minutes, then interrupted him. 'You like me, Mr Englewood, hey? You don't read so good? You got the book down side upwards!'

Inside the bedroom Sara wasted no time. She spread out the syringes on the little table, set up the bottle of insulin, and tossed the orange on to the bed.

'Now, George,' she said, 'Listen carefully. There are lots of diabetics in the world. It won't be a problem to you if you follow the rules. You require one shot every morning, and you have to do it for yourself. That's the hard part!'

Then she carefully drilled him in the procedure, using water and an old needle, giving injections to the orange. After he had demonstrated ten times his ability to do the job, she laid out the insulin, alcohol, and the package of sterile disposable needles.

'Okay, champ,' she smiled, 'now here's where we go for broke. You know all the places to use, but for this test we'll use the fatty tissue on the calf of your right leg. Drop the pants, load the needle, and go for broke!'

Five minutes later, after a near-perfect drill, George looked up at her with relief. 'It didn't hurt a bit, Sara,' he said. 'Not a bit! I was scared to death.'

'Yes, everybody is, George,' she congratulated him. 'It takes more courage to inject yourself than it does to run off left tackle. Now remember, use each needle once—use it, then break it up like this, and throw it away. Okay, young man, the lessons are over. And tomorrow you fly on your own.'

The boy stood up and pulled up his trousers. He walked with Sara to the door as she opened it. She stretched up to kiss him on his cheek, and he walked out, grinning broadly, still stuffing his shirt into his trousers.

'I'll be out in a minute,' Sara called from behind him in the bedroom. 'I have to clean up.'

'Ah, George,' his father greeted the boy with a bear-hug, 'is not so bad as you think, no?' The two of them walked towards the door, then he stopped. 'Hey, Sara,' he called, 'I forgot for to pay you, no?'

'This one's on the house,' Sara called from the bedroom.

'Now what I tell you, Mr Englewood?' Henry Gomez grinned. 'No fuss, no trouble, no nothin'! What I tell you, that Sara knows her business, you bet. I bet you never see nothing like this before!'

'I bet you a million dollars I haven't!' John Englewood muttered as the door closed behind them.

CHAPTER TWO

SARA was whistling as she walked out of the bedroom. 'Sorry about that,' she said. 'Would you like another cup of coffee?' John shook his head. Somehow he had changed, and she wondered why. 'Then if you'll excuse me again, I'll go up in the loft and get you some more blankets. I just put fresh sheets on the bed.'

'That's—nice of you, Sara. May I use your telephone for a few minutes? I need to check up on things at home.'

She waved him permission.

'It's in the bedroom,' she said, and started up the stairs. Halfway up she had another thought, and turned. 'Mr Englewood—John? When you use the——' She stopped in mid-sentence. He had already gone into the bedroom and closed the door behind him. 'And a lot of good that'll do you,' Sara chuckled. 'You can be heard all over the house, no matter how many doors you shut!' She resumed her whistling way up to search through her linen shelves.

When John picked up the telephone downstairs she could actually hear him dialling, so much like a sound-duct was the layout of the house. A moment later she heard his booming voice.

'Robert? Can you hear me now? This is a terrible line—speak a little louder, please. What are you doing at the farm?' There was a spaced silence. 'Oh, my God! All last night? Hysterics, I suppose? What did Doctor Feinberg say?' Another silence. 'But how about tonight? We can't just keep feeding the kid pills!' Another silence. 'All right, Robert, I'll come home tonight. Yes, at once. The girl? Yes, I found the girl. A tiny little thing, looks to be about sixteen or seventeen. No family around here, both her parents dead. Yes, I put the proposal to her, Robert.' His voice lowered slightly. He

28

sounded weary, overset by cares. 'I know you think it's terribly important, Robert, but I don't. And if we take her on we're really taking on a can of worms. No, don't kid yourself. She looks as if butter wouldn't melt in her mouth, but you can feel behind it all she's got a spine of steel. And that's not all she's got. She also comes equipped with a baby about a year or eighteen months old, I guess. She tells me she works nights downtown in New Bedford. Yes, I'm sure you've heard of the place— a fishing town, a tough place. What?' A pregnant silence followed. 'Come on, Robert! I sat here tonight and watched while she pulled a trick with a fifteen-year-old kid. Do I have to draw you a picture? The girl's a hooker! I said she's a hooker—a prostitute!'

It was at that point that Sara shut off her ears. For several minutes she hid in the loft, trying to regain control of her dignity and her shattered nerves. She sat down on her bed, cradling the blankets in her arms, casting back in her mind, trying to see the events of the day as John had seen them. And when she did, her anger fled. She was giggling as she thumped down the stairs. She hesitated near the bottom of the staircase, just out of range of the light of the lamp, and schooled her face into cautious dignity.

He was standing at the kitchen door, puffing at a cigarette. When he saw her he stubbed it out and threw the butt into the garbage can.

'I'll have your bed ready in a few minutes,' she offered, trying to avoid looking at him.

'I don't think that will be necessary,' he returned. 'I've just had some disturbing news from home.'

'Yes, I know,' she retorted. 'I could hear you all over the house.' She sidled by him and went into the bedroom, using the excuse of bedmaking to gain more time. He followed her. 'You heard everything?' he asked.

'Almost,' she replied, stiff-lipped.

He grabbed her by the wrists and pulled her out to the dining table. She came reluctantly, forcing him to apply some pressure to drag her along. He shifted his grip from her wrists to her shoulders, and pushed her down into one of the straight-backed chairs. Sara sat quietly, both feet flat on the floor, hands folded in her lap, back stiff as a ramrod.

'It isn't true, you know,' she said quietly.

'I want you to listen to me, Sara,' he said. She looked up at him, and squeezed her lips tight shut. John leaned over as if to shake something out of her, but stopped as she flinched away from him. He straightened up again, ran a hand through his hair, and unloosened his necktie.

'I don't have any good apologies, Sara,' he said, 'and I'm not your judge. But I do have a terrible problem, and I need your help. May I explain?'

She continued to look at him without speaking. Her lips were pressed hard together. To him it looked to be in anger; to her it was because it was the only way she could control the giggles. 'Damn you, Sara!' he sighed. He took one of the other chairs in hand, turned it around backwards, and straddled it, using its back as a place to rest his forearms. 'I'm going to tell you anyway,' he stated. 'And you're going to listen.' He pounded the top of the chair with his clenched fist. 'Why does it all have to come at once?' he despaired. 'I haven't had a minute's sleep in forty-eight hours. We're in trouble on the farm. The gypsy moths are in the apple orchards, and it looks as if we'll lose the entire crop. And then the factory. For some reason I don't understand, the more orders we get the more money we lose. But that's just worrisome. The real problem is my son. He's seven—no, eight years old; you heard me on the telephone. I've been away for two days, and he's running wild with hysterics. The doctor finally had to give him tranquillisers, just because he can't find me. When I'm at home he follows me around like a puppy. He doesn't want anything from me, he just wants to see that I'm still there.'

He paused for a moment to wipe his forehead. Almost automatically his hand moved to his pocket for a cigarette. Sara made no complaint as he lit up and drew a deep drag of smoke into his lungs.

'There has to be a reason,' she suggested, her voice soft and soothing.

'Oh God!' he laughed ruefully. 'There are plenty of reasons. His mother and I used to fight like cats and dogs. There never was a moment of peace.' He drew on his cigarette again.

'But that's not hardly enough to drive a normal child to hysterics, John,' she said.

'No? Perhaps Jack isn't a normal child. Perhaps—oh hell, you might as well hear it all.' He made to throw his butt into an ashtray, but could find none. Sara reached over and took it from him.

'Two years ago, Sara, I was conducting a night seminar at the University. Amherst, where the University is located, is about six miles away from our house in South Deerfield. Jackie was at home with Elena. Nobody else was in the house. Somehow or another Elena fell down the front stairs. She was dead when I got home. She was dead, lying at the foot of the stairs, and Jackie was sitting on the floor next to her, crying his heart out, and yelling 'Don't leave me, Mamma!' Those words have haunted me ever since!' He lifted one of his massive fingers and pushed away a tear. 'They told me she'd been dead for three hours before I got there, and all that time the boy was sitting there, trying to wake her up!'

'But surely, in two years, things have got better?'

'Of course they have. We've had him to every shrink in the county. He's calmed down considerably, but still in the back of his mind he has this thing. And I'm all he has left, I guess, so he means to cling even closer to me.' John paused again, the look of hurt deep-lined in his face. Sara felt the crazy urge to reach out to comfort him, but before she could think seriously about it, her traitor hand had wandered across the space between them and gently finger-walked through his hair. After a moment he reached up and gently pulled her hand down to his lips.

'Well,' he sighed, getting up from the chair, 'those are my problems. I don't know really why I told you all that.'

'You have to tell *somebody*,' she replied. 'And now me. Am I another one of your problems? Am I going to be the straw that broke the——'

'No, Sara, no!' he exclaimed. 'Not you. You're not a problem. In fact, you might be a solution. After all, you're not so old yourself. Yes——' he held up both hands in a form of surrender, 'yes, I know you're older than I think, but perhaps you would be willing to help with Jackie? We have plenty of help in the house to keep it going. I have a live-in housekeeper, a girl who comes every day to do the cleaning, and a middle-aged couple who actually run the farm. And then there's my son.'

'And your brother Robert?'

'Oh, him—he doesn't actually live at the house. He's the President of our plant, and has his own pad. And that's the total of our family. Come along with me, Sara. That way at least we can have all our troubles in one place!'

He had been pacing up and down all this time, but stopped short and turned around towards her. 'Damn!' he snorted. 'That wasn't terribly diplomatic, was it? Will you come, Sara?'

She stood up, walked over to him, and put her arms around his waist. She snuggled up to him, trying to bring comfort by body contact. Her nose rested on the fourth button of his shirt, and her head almost fitted into his armpit. A comfortable fit, she thought. More comfort for me than for him?

'Yes, John, I'll come,' she said. 'If you'd told me about the boy earlier there would never have been a doubt. I like children. But don't forget that Mary has to come too. Suppose we give it a trial—a thirty-day free trial? But if I do come, you must remember that I intend to be me!'

He pushed her back away slightly, hands on her shoulders. 'Be whoever you please, Sara,' he said gruffly. 'Bring the dog, bring the baby, bring whatever you please. The only thing I ask of you is that when you get up there you'll just not practise your—profession—for a while. A deal?'

She smiled up at him. 'Yes, a deal. But not the baby. Pudge has to stay here. His father is coming for him tomorrow.'

'His father? You two are on friendly terms?'

'Why, of course we are. He's a fine man!'

'And you don't mind leaving the child with his father for six months or more?'

'Why should I? He's married, you know. Sylvia, his wife, is a wonderful woman.'

'And she's willing to take this child into her home?'

'Willing? She's crazy about Pudge! I don't understand you.'

'I guess I don't understand you either, Sara. I must seem like a Babe in the Woods to you. Okay, so you leave the baby here. But I have to go back tonight. Why don't you pack up, and tomorrow, after I've snatched a couple of hours of sleep, I'll come back and get you. Unless you could go with me tonight?'

'I can't, tonight. Ralph is coming tomorrow. And then I want to say goodbye to all the people here at the Point. But that's quite a distance to drive, isn't it? You must live close to two hundred miles from here.'

'Not quite. About a hundred and forty-five, as the crow flies.'

'But I have a car,' she offered. 'A 1967 Volkswagen Bug. I could drive myself.'

'Nonsense, Sara—I'll come to get you. You're not going to arrive in our part of the country unescorted. I'll be back some time after lunch. You be packed and ready.'

'You know something?' she said, a speculative smile on her face. 'You give orders just the way my brothers all did. Snap to it, little female!'

'I'm accustomed to being in charge of things,' John laughed. 'There's nothing can change that particular aspect of me. Are you one of these liberated women?'

Sara avoided the challenge. 'I really think it's sort of

nice,' she said primly, 'to have a man who knows what he wants, and doesn't have to be wishy-washy about it at all. Of course, liberated or not, I'm one of those women who really don't care to receive orders!'

John smiled back at her, eyes twinkling. Why, he's almost handsome, Sara thought. Almost—and then her thoughts were blotted out as he swung her up off the ground to his own level, and gently kissed her. When he put her down again she clung for a moment, breathless. He walked her to the door, his arm around her shoulders, hers around his waist. As he went out on to the porch and stopped, she called after him.

'John,' she asked, 'after what you said about me—after what you think, why did you kiss me?'

'I don't know Sara for Short,' he said. 'I guess—just because I wanted to. See you tomorrow!' and he strode out of sight around the back of the house, leaving Sara alone in the dark world. Only the flash of the Butlers Flat beacon and the clang of the bell-buoy that marked the channel up the bay consoled her. She shivered, knowing deep in her mind that this had been a day to mark a sea-change in her life.

All in all, she spent a restless, sleepless night. She tossed and turned in her extra-wide bed, but found no comfort. When the wind came up, about two in the morning, she stumbled downstairs to check on Pudge and the windows, then fumbled her way back to bed. The baby made his usual morning noises at six-thirty, just after she had finally got to sleep. The morning had come damp with fog; she could hear the heavy blasts of the foghorn on the sea-dyke protecting New Bedford harbour. She shivered in her thin nightgown, but hurried down the stairs to rescue Pudge from his playpen.

They carried on a conversation together as she made breakfast, he perched securely on her hip, playing with her braids. They both had a great deal to say to each other, none of it intelligible. The baby bathed in his porridge, and ate a little. Sara nibbled a piece of toast and wondered if she might venture an egg without bursting her seams. It was almost impossible for her to turn her mind from the strange man who had intruded on her life, given her her marching orders, and then vanished into the night. 'It might be nice,' she told Pudge dreamily, 'to be—what's the word?—cossetted? For just a little while, of course! He thinks I'm a child, a wanton child at that. And yet he kissed me! I never could understand you men, Pudge,' she told her nephew. 'But since he thinks I'm just a kid, we'd better get some just-a-kid clothes. And they'll have to be loose, because I just don't have a little-girl bust. And therefore, Master Anderson,' she said with a flourish, 'there's no real reason why I shouldn't have an egg, is there?'

At which Master Anderson gurgled with such a serious and devilishly logical answer that she had three, fried in butter, with shavings of cheese and tomato mixed in. And the last bit of Portuguese Linguica which had been haunting the refrigerator. It was all very satisfactory indeed.

When her brother Ralph arrived, about eight o'clock, she had Pudge and all his things packed. The little man rolled across the floor towards his father with great glee, shouting 'Mamma!' at the top of his voice.

'Oh, it's good to see you, Ralph,' she gasped, after he had swung her around three or four times and given her a compound rib fracture. 'Put me down, you big ox! How's Sylvia?'

'She's in good shape, Sara,' he replied. 'The operation on her eye was a complete success. She'll be released from the hospital tomorrow, and we should be able to get into our new home in Hyannis by next Tuesday. How's Pudge been?'

'He's been fine,' she reported. 'As good as gold. And I think he's grown an inch or more. He's walking much better! You'll see. He loves to paddle in the ocean.'

'That's fine, Sara. Pudge and I will drive to Boston today, and bail Mamma out of the hospital tomorrow. We're going to have three or four days before we move into the house. Suppose you make us reservations at the Inn for from tomorrow on—say, about four days minimum?'

'Ralph,' she giggled, 'I've got a better idea. Why don't you and Sylvia come here to the cottage and spend a couple of weeks? It's cold, but it's sunny. All my jonquils are still blooming, and you could mind my house for me. Would you?'

'And just where will you be, little sister, that somebody has to mind your house for you?' His voice had that suspicious "what's Sara up to now" tone about it, the natural suspicion of a thirty-seven-year-old brother with a twenty-four-year-old baby sister.

'I don't really know how to explain it all, Ralph,' she answered, 'but do you remember that elderly lady who used to share the beach with me, the one I called Aunt Cindy? Well, somehow or another she died, and left me in her will.'

'You must have misunderstood, Sara. People don't get left in wills. Things get left. Did she leave you something in her will?'

She giggled in his ear. 'No, Ralph, I know exactly what I'm saying. She didn't really leave me anything. She left me in her will—to her nephew. And last night he came down from South Deerfield to claim his inheritance!'

'Sara,' he complained, 'for twenty-two years I've been trying to understand you. Up until you were two years old I had you figured out, but since then you've eluded me. Now start again slowly, from the beginning, and tell me the whole story!'

Which she did, leaving out the sections about what John had called her, and—for some reason that she could not herself understand, the part about being kissed, and feeling a flame run up and down her spine whenever he touched her, and really how handsome he was—in an ugly sort of way, and—'And that's why, and I'm going,' she finished primly.

To which her oldest brother, who really hadn't a clue where women were concerned—except for Sylvia, of course—gave up the argument, kissed her soundly, threatened that he would call David in Dallas (because David knew *all* about women,) and climbed back into his car. But before he left, he got in one parting shot. 'And keep your nose out of their business, Sara. If ever there was a real nosy parker, you're it! And take that crazy dog with you. Maybe Mary will be able to keep you out of trouble, that is if she doesn't fall over her own feet!'

'Don't you insult my dog, you homely overgrown chauvinist!' she yelled after him as his car spurted down the dirt track towards the main road. And then she laughed, fell down on the sand beside Mary, and hugged her—and thought as she did how nice it was to be a woman, and to have big brothers to call upon if needed.

She went back into the cottage to give it a lick and a promise for Sylvia's sake, but at nine o'clock she wandered up the beach to the Brashers' cottage, and her last morning coffee with the Point Judith Chowder and Marching Society. Which was the name they all assigned to the informal meetings of most of the year-round residents of the Point. The coffee was good, the doughnuts were superb, and for once Sara was the bearer of the most exciting item of gossip. They passed an hour in friendship. 'But you can't go away,' moaned Henry Brasher, seventeen, and known to his family as the most brash of the Brashers. 'You can't go away! It's almost summer, and I've fallen in love with you, and what will I do for a date?'

'You'll think of something, Henry,' she assured him. 'And besides, a girl my age has to begin thinking about marriage. Just what are your intentions, Harry?' At which the young man withdrew under a barrage of catcalls, the last doughnut was divided, the last goodbye given, every male in the room had been kissed, and Sara started back home.

Harry Burton, the retired union organiser, walked her down the beach to her own porch, with Mary padding at her side. He held her tiny hand for a moment, his white thin hair ruffled by the small breeze that was moving the fog away. 'Don't ever forget, Sara baby,' he said, 'that we'll all be here. If you need us, you call. There isn't a family on the Point that you haven't done something good for. Don't forget, call if you need help. We owe you.'

She barely managed to stammer an answer before he kissed her gently on the forehead, then patted Mary on the head. 'And you, you miserable fake, stick close and watch over her, you hear?' At which the dog, not at all put out by the words, growled. Then Harry was gone, making his last goodbye.

Halfway buried in her dream fantasies, Sara went in to pack. She muddled through her wardrobe, abandoning all but one of her nurse's uniforms, and concentrating mainly on slacks, loose skirts, and separate blouses. Her hand wandered once to her favourite evening gown, but she reluctantly put it back. Then she crammed into the case her favourite passions: filmy nightgowns and exotic lace bikini panties. She skipped her few lace half-bras; she only wore bras to formal affairs, anyway. By the time she had struggled downstairs, it was twelve o'clock. She heard the whisper of his car as he drove up. 'Young Lochinvar rides out of the West,' she giggled to Mary, but there was a thought niggling at the back of her mind. 'But it never said that he *married* the fair maiden, did it?' Mary ignored the comment, and walked towards the door. Sara followed.

He came in without knocking. She held out both her hands to him, and smiled up at him. He looked more rested, more at ease, and his dark eyes sparkled at her. 'Well now, that's the kind of welcome a man needs!' he chuckled. He leaned down and gently brushed a kiss across her forehead. 'Everybody at home is waiting for you. Decided to take the baby with you?'

She shook her head at him, swinging her long free hair across her back. When she had come back from the party she had remembered his comment about her hair at the dinner table, and so she had unbraided it, combed it out carefully, and fastened it lightly into a ponytail, tying it back with a little red ribbon. She had dressed more carefully, too, without being willing to admit to herself why she had done it. Her white cord slacks were loose, because of the weight she had lost in that long ordeal of nursing her mother. But the yellow dimity blouse left nothing to the imagination. She had covered it with a bright red windbreaker.

'I told you last night,' she said, 'Pudge has gone off with his father. We're all there is, Mary and me and two suitcases.'

'Mary and I,' John said absentmindedly.

'Yes,' she answered solemnly. 'What you said.'

He squeezed her arm gently, then stood aside as she coaxed Mary into the back seat. When they were both seated and buckled up he sat watching her, a curious expression on his face. He smiled again, as if the thought were pleasant. Then he turned the ignition key on the heavy sedan and backed down the long sandy path until he reached the only paved highway on the Point. He stopped the car there. 'Here's where we begin a new life, Sara. I like your hair that way, but it makes you look even younger. Now keep your chin up, and learn to enjoy!' He reached over and patted her knee. She felt like saying 'Yes, Daddy,' but refrained. When John looked over his left shoulder to check for oncoming traffic, she could not hold back. She crinkled up her nose and stuck out her tongue. He looked back just in time to catch her in that ridiculous position.

'Something on your tongue?' he enquired.

'I was just looking to see if it was still heavily coated,' she lied. Her conscience made a note of it. She settled her hands demurely in her lap and paid careful attention to the scenery, which she had seen a thousand times before. John drove the heavy car off the Point and climbed up on Route I-195 at the Marion exit.

'I need to make one stop—please?' she asked. He nodded. 'Two exits down. Just as you come off the highway there's a shopping plaza.'

'Okay. Did you have breakfast?'

'Yes, I did. The neighbours gave me a breakfast farewell. Everybody came.'

'Is this the plaza?' he asked, slowing down.

'Yes. If you could drive over there to the entrance to King's department store, please. I'll be about ten minutes.'

She climbed out of the car as soon as it came to a stop. 'Mary! Stay!' she commanded. The big dog, who had not appeared to be making any plans at all to get out, barely opened an eye and winked. Sara stalked off, muttering under her breath.

Inside the uncrowded store she went directly to the section devoted to off-the-rack dresses, found the rack carrying dresses one size too large for her, and snatched at random for six A-line summer-pattern shifts. She made no attempt at colour co-ordination. In fact, one that came in her favourite yellow, with bluebell patterns, she rejected and returned to the rack. The counter attendant was amazed when Sara insisted that all but one be rolled up in a bundle and compressed into a plastic shopping bag. The one remaining she took with her into the store's skimpy changing room and put it on, stuffing her slacks and blouse into the sack on top of the new clothes. Then she shrugged her windbreaker over the whole awful concoction and went back out to the car.

'First time I've ever waited "just ten minutes" for a woman and found her back in the prescribed time,' John commented. 'Oh—a dress? I thought——'

'It's only proper, when you're meeting new people, for a woman to wear a dress,' Sara stated rather matter-of-factly. 'That's what Mamma always said.'

'Ah, of course. And your mother knew, because she was a surgeon?'

'If you're being sarcastic, Mr Englewood, you're wasting your time. My mother knew everything there was to know about being a woman. And she always told me that was enough to know. For a girl to try to know or understand a man, she told me, was like trying to swim up Niagara Falls on Christmas Day.'

'I give up!' he apologised, raising both hands in surrender. 'Your mother was probably right. We'll talk about it some other time. Fasten your seatbelt, Sara.'

'It won't fasten,' she complained, struggling with the heavy buckle. John reached over with both hands, twisted the belt slightly, and she heard the buckle snick home without trouble. But in the doing his right arm brushed against her breast and remained there for just a moment, dimpling its soft fullness with his weight. He seemed to pay no attention, but Sara felt a shock of startling proportion course up through her body, and then down again to her stomach. She sat, not breathing, while he turned the ignition key again and they rolled out on to the highway.

About fifty feet down the road he took one hand off the steering wheel and shook her shoulder gently. 'Breathe, Sara,' he coaxed. 'I do believe you're turning blue! My driving isn't that bad!'

She shrugged her shoulders, then pulled herself into as small a bundle as she could and huddled against the opposite door. 'Hunker down!' That was another expression of her mother's. 'When the wild Indians of the world attack, pull your wagon train into a circle, and hunker down!' Sara hunkered, wondering fiercely how he could be so casually driving down the highway after such a momentous encounter. Well, it would be a long drive to South Deerfield. She would huddle in the corner and not say another word about anything. 'But I do so wish I understood men,' she muttered, half to herself.

'Hmm?' he enquired. 'What did you say, Sara?'

'I said——' she stammered, then looked out her side window in alarm. 'I said you are taking the wrong turn. You don't get off at this exit. You stay on I-195 until you get to Providence!'

'Yes, well,' he agreed, looking over his shoulder at the merging traffic, 'I don't doubt that you do. But I don't.'

Sara still had her mouth half open as he drove down the off ramp at the New Bedford exit, and shortly thereafter pulled into the tiny parking place of the New Bedford airport. He climbed out, stretched his legs, and went to the back of the car for their luggage.

'You'll have to leash the dog,' he said as he opened the door for her.

'Oh? I—well, I do have a travelling leash. Mary and I have travelled a great deal together, you know.'

'Is that so?' he enquired, busy about his tasks, and casual. 'All the way to Boston, I suppose?'

Mary stood still while Sara attached a shoulder harness with a projecting handle, much like that of a seeing-eye dog. 'Oh yes,' she said very solemnly. 'We went to Boston, and Providence, and Worcester, and Leominster——' and then under her breath, 'and Heidelberg and Rome and Athens and Tokyo. And wouldn't that spin your gourd, Mr Know-it-all!'

'Hmm?' he asked.

'Oh, nothing,' she replied. 'The buckle was hard to fasten.'

'Come on, then,' said John. He led the way through the tiny passenger lounge, filled out some papers at the flight desk, and conducted her out on to the concrete taxiway. She followed along without argument, outwardly placid, but inwardly quaking. An attendant started to say something when he saw the dog, but then shrugged his shoulders. Sara giggled and hurried after her escort. Like a dinghy in the wake of an Island steamer, she told herself. If there was anything she needed to teach this man besides humility, it would be how to walk slower!

He led her directly to a small aircraft parked on the flight line. 'A cessna 175,' he commented, answering her query. 'It's an old model, but very dependable. A company plane, of course.'

'Of course,' she squeaked, trying to hide her astonishment. 'Doesn't everyone?'

'Doesn't everyone what?' he asked as he stepped up on the landing gear pad and opened the hatch.

'Doesn't everyone have a company airplane?' Sara finished her sentence lamely. The situation was getting completely out of hand. The smallest plane that Sara had ever been in had been a 747 jumbo jet, and the thought of flying in this little—kite—weakened her knees considerably. She tried to hide her fears as best she could behind her sunniest little-girl smile. It seemed to work. The furrow disappeared from his forehead and he smiled back at her. He stepped back down on to the tarmac.

'If I pick her up will she bite?' he asked.

'Who, me?' she stuttered. 'I don't bite—well, not very often, I mean.'

'I'm glad to hear that,' he said dryly. 'The dog. I mean the dog. If I pick her up will she bite? Unless you think she would jump up as high as this sill?'

'Well, probably not,' she stammered. 'Mary isn't very good at jumping into strange airplanes. To tell the truth, Mr Englewood——'

'John,' he interrupted. 'Call me John, please.'

'Very well—John,' she repeated. 'I should tell you something about Mary. She's a sort of fake, you know. She growls very efficiently, and she might gum you a bit if you tried to hurt me, but beyond that she's a semi- retired fake. If you go about it very slowly she might not be insulted. But she weighs eighty-four pounds, you know.'

Having spent many a day trying to pick Mary up herself, Sara was a trifle disconcerted to see this man slide both arms under Mary's belly and deposit her in the hatchway like a carton of beer. And then he turned to her.

'Oh—no!' she protested, still with the squeak in her voice. 'I think I could climb up there very nicely. Besides, I weigh a hundred and seven pounds and a——' and I don't want you to put your arms around me and disturb my very precarious peace of mind any more than you have, was what she wanted to say, but she was too late. John grinned at her, a facial change that completely rewrote her concept of good looks and personality. Then he swept her up, holding her closely, and set her down with her feet inside the fuselage. 'Watch your head,' he warned as he shut the door securely behind her.

Never mind my head, she shouted at herself, watch your heart! And then to him, 'I thought you were just a schoolteacher, not a weight-lifter!' She was trying to smooth her skirts down around her, and at the same time regain some control over her errant emotions.

'Right on both counts,' John called up to her. 'Try to get Mary settled down between those middle seats, and then strap yourself in. I have to make a pre-flight inspection.'

Sara watched him as he walked slowly around the outside of the plane, looking closely at his checkpoints. When he had completed the entire walk-around he climbed into the left-hand front seat beside her. When he had settled into the seat he ran his eyes carefully over the instrument panel, made an adjustment to a little crank just overhead, and pressed the starter button on the engine. As the heavy propeller in front of them kicked over and began to purr at them, he turned to her and smiled.

'Almost ready!' he yelled above the engine noise. Then he looked backward, carefully manoeuvring the rudder and ailerons for their final check.

Sara reached over and punched his arm to get his attention. He had been about ready to don a pair of headphones, but he stopped and looked at her.

'Is the pilot coming,' she gasped, afraid to hear the answer, but even more afraid not to ask.

'I'm the pilot,' he announced casually. 'He's me—I am he, or whatever.'

'Yes, of course,' Sara squeaked, 'whatever!' And wondered if she had time to unbuckle, open the door, and run all the way back to Point Judith before he said another word!

CHAPTER THREE

As she looked back on it, Sara realised that that forty-minute flight might not have been the worst time in her life. But during the flight itself she was not so sure. She had sat rigidly straight in her seat, both hands grasping the seat itself, from the moment they taxied out to the runway, until the engine had finally shut down at the end of the trip. Her fingers were stiff, their tips slightly blue. The little plane had bounced most uncomfortably, and her stomach continuously sent up complaints about uneasy travel. She was staring out at the startling blue of a large lake when the plane seemed to fall out from under her. She shrieked, and then it bounced back up.

'We're going to crash!' she yelled, reaching for the door handle. 'We'd better get out!'

'You bet,' John yelled back at her. 'We're only flying at three thousand feet. Get your hands off that door!' It was then that she noticed that the arrogant monster was actually laughing at her. Laughing at her!

'Updraughts and downdraughts,' he explained. 'They come about when the hills and water are warmed at different rates by the sun. Nothing to worry about. That's Quabban Reservoir down below us, the water supply for the Boston metropolitan area. Now all we have to do is make it over this little ridge of hills, and—voila—the Connecticut River valley. Hang on!'

At that point the right wing of the plane dropped almost out of sight as they banked to turn north. Lucky I'm already mad at him, Sara told herself grimly. He's bouncing this thing around on purpose. And I won't forget it. Hang on? She said a quick 'Hail Mary,' and looked down at her hands. The knuckles were turning from white to blue. If I hang on any tighter, she told herself, I'll pull the seat right off the floor!

To take her mind off of her own troubles she squirmed around in her seat to see how Mary was making out. To her intense disgust the great black cowardly monster was fast asleep. When Sara turned frontward again she was seized in absolute terror. The plane was diving straight down towards a cluster of farms and roads. 'But there's no airport!' she screamed at him.

'Did you suppose I was going to land in the river?' he asked. 'And will you stop beating my arm for a moment! I do need two hands. The airstrip is right in front of you.'

'Oh well—I was just trying to help!' Sara sniffed at him and tossed her head to show her complete indifference to anything he might do. Not only pompous, but bossy and sarcastic too, she noted. But as she watched him manoeuvre she could not help but think, He must be a little younger than I thought earlier. Those eyebrows aren't really all that heavy—although they do really meet in the middle. What would he say if she were to reach over and ruffle them? Her hand was already moving in his direction when, out of the corner of her eye, she noticed that the ground was coming up at them with tremendous speed. She grabbed the edges of her seat again, hunched her shoulders, and said two more 'Hail Marys' with both eyes squeezed shut. By the time she had finished the plane was on the ground, rolling without trouble along a grass landing strip. Hoping that John had not noticed, she opened both eyes, forced her fingers to unclench, leaned back in her seat, and gave a hearty sigh of relief. The plane taxied off the grass runway and up on to a concrete parking pad. The motor died, the propeller grumbled to a stop, and he set the brakes.

Then he reached over towards her with a handkerchief, and wiped the perspiration from her brow. 'You had a tough flight, Sara,' he said solicitously. 'Too bad you didn't come with me!' He was laughing at her again, she knew, but her stomach was too upset, and bile blocked her quick retort. I'll get you for this, John Englewood, she promised herself. You just watch! I'll get even with you!

John seemed unmoved by the terrible threat that hung over his head. He climbed out of the plane, came around to her side, and lifted her down to the ground with practised ease. Mary watched them both from the open door as they stood close together, his arms still around Sara, supporting her as she gingerly tried to get her legs to hold her up. He was still laughing as he leaned down and kissed her. She squeaked again, and pulled away from him. 'Come on, you damn guard dog,' she hissed under her breath, 'jump down here and bite him!'

But Mary had other thoughts. The dog measured the distance, jumped to the ground, and sauntered past them both as if they were strangers. John took Sara's arm and pulled her around in front of him. As if he were reading her mind he said, 'It's *man's* best friend, you know.' Before she could think of a suitable reply he led her around the wing towards the waiting jeep.

'Sara, this is Frank Stankiewicz,' he said, presenting a middle-aged and well set-up man standing beside the vehicle. 'Frank runs the farm, Sara.' Then, to the man, 'If you don't mind, Frank, Sara needs some lunch. Could you tie down the plane and make the checks? I'll send the jeep back for you in a few minutes.'

'No trouble at all, John,' the farmer returned. 'You'd better get along. They sent Jackie back from school about fifteen minutes ago.'

'And we could have done without that!' John replied. Brusquely he encouraged Mary into the back seat of the vehicle, then gave Sara a hand up into the high front seat. He climbed in on the driver's side and gunned the vehicle down the gravelled lane that led from the airstrip to the rambling farmhouse about a quarter of a mile away. The movement, and the wind in her face, restored Sara's good humour. She would not, she decided, murder him today.

'It's an old house,' John shouted at her. 'The original parts were built around 1720, but there've been six separate additions. You can see by the different roof levels where each new addition was tucked on to the previous buildings. The corridors have steps in them, because the additions were not all at the same level. And a few unexpected turns, too. But the roof doesn't leak, the kitchen is modern, we've put in central heat, and the Englewoods have lived here since 1746. I think you'll like it.'

'I'm sure I will,' she shouted back. 'It looks grand. I love these old clapboard houses. And wooden shutters for every window? And what are those strange looking barns behind the house?'

'Those tall skinny barns are the drying sheds. We hang the tobacco leaf in there to cure it. Our two main crops out here, Sara—cigar tobacco from the flatlands along the river, and apples from the orchards up on the hillsides. And then Frank keeps pigs, and Mrs Emory keeps chickens. In another two weeks you'll be able to smell the apple blossoms. You can't help but love that.'

The jeep swept around the back side of the house, past a long low garage, and came to a halt before the front porch, a real veranda that swept across the entire front of the house, and disappeared around the unseen side.

'Okay now, Sara,' he admonished as he helped her out. 'Chin up! We've met the enemy and they're us. Let's go in.'

He was laughing again, but Sara could see nothing funny about the whole affair. Now that they had arrived, she was petrified. She tried to smooth her wrinkled dress, then gave it up with the vague notion that perhaps she could do something about her windblown hair. And all the time her mind was running around a circular track. Why had Aunt Cindy made such a will? Was it the little boy who needed her? Or John himself? Or that other unknown quantity, Robert? Perhaps she had better keep notes on all of them. Including herself? Did Aunt Cindy think *she* had a problem? She shook her totally confused head, practised her smile for a second or two, then followed him up the stairs to the broad veranda. She kept her hand on Mary's head as she walked, seeking confidence from contact.

She had hardly adjusted her eyes to the darkness of the hall when she received her first surprise. Two people were waiting for them, one an elderly woman whose huge smile and well-rounded figure seemed to say 'housekeeper', the other a small boy with pinched cheeks and a scowling face, whose thin body seemed to say 'trouble!' The boy took one look at Sara and ducked behind the housekeeper's skirts. Sara reached out for the handle of Mary's leash and waited for some one to say something. It was John who broke the silence.

'Mrs Emory, this is Sara. She's hungry and could use considerable feeding up. Would you do that?'

The woman stepped forward and put her arms around Sara. It was like stepping into a warm heart. Although not tall, she stood a good two inches above Sara, and enveloped her more than hugged her. 'Welcome home, Sara,' she said. 'John told us about you last night. Why don't you have a word or two with Jack, here, while I go rustle up a few things in the kitchen?' With one hand she drew the boy around in front of her. 'And there's a telephone call for you in the library, John. Robert is holding.'

John smiled at them, turned left, and closed the library door behind him. Mrs Emory went down the hall, turned right through the swinging door under the wide mahogany staircase, and disappeared into the kitchen.

The boy stood frozen in position, glaring at Sara through hate-filled eyes. She could see some vague resemblance between the child and his father. Jack had the same dark hair, but where the father's was a riot of curls, the son's lay smooth and straight across his forehead. His eyes were a gleaming grey-green. With his narrow face and pained expression he looked like a trapped fox.

'Oh lordy,' thought Sara, 'here is the problem!' But she mustered up her courage and stuck out her hand in welcome. 'Hi, Jack,' she said, 'I'm Sara.'

The boy looked suspiciously at the offered hand, then casually reached out to grab it with his own. But instead of giving it a gentle shake, he pulled her hand up to his mouth and bit hard on the tender junction between her thumb and finger. A surge of pain shot up through Sara's hand and arm. She jerked the hand back with a muffled exclamation of pain. Tears flushed her eyes. She stifled the urge to club the little monster, and muttered a couple of unladylike words under her breath, wondering what to do next—but Mary saved the day with her own answer.

The big dog padded forward two paces and stood head to head with the boy. The child seemed to freeze again, a wary look on his face. Mary considered him for a moment, then stretched out her immense tongue and licked his face with a slobbering sweeping motion.

'Who—who's he?' the boy whispered.

'She's my guard dog,' Sara said quietly.

'What does he guard?' The boy's voice was fraught with doubt.

'Me,' said Sara.

'What does he do if he gets mad?'

'He only gets mad if somebody tries to hurt me.'

'And then?'

'And then he eats them!'

The boy paused to think the situation over. Mary continued to lick him with her rough tongue.

'What's she doing now?' the boy whispered.

'Tasting you. She likes to taste people before she eats them. But I suppose she'll give you a second chance. Better be careful, though. If you were to bite me again I'm afraid Mary will eat you. Want to bite me again?' She offered her injured hand.

'No—no, thank you,' the boy replied. 'It was a mistake.'

'Yes, wasn't it? Sit, Mary!' Both the boy and Sara were surprised to see the big dog sink to its haunches. Probably the beast had already decided to sit down, Sara thought.

'Are you going to tell my father?' the boy asked.

'Am I going to get bit again?' she asked. The boy shook his head and mustered a tiny smile.

'Well, in that case—hi, Jack. My name is Sara.' She extended her hand again.

He took it, with one eye on the dog, and shook it gently.

'I'm pleased to meet you, Sara,' he said, 'Aren't I?'

'I suppose we both are, Jack,' Sara chuckled. 'Pleased, I mean.'

'But if you do it I'll bite you again,' the boy said solemnly. 'And I don't care if your dog eats me.'

'Do it?' Sara asked. 'Do what?'

'You came to take my dad away from me. If you do I'll bite you again—you better believe me!'

'Oh, I believe you, Jack. But you better believe me, too. I didn't come to take your dad away from you. I wouldn't think of doing that. Who told you such a thing?'

'He did. He said you'd come and live with us so you could make my daddy like you and then you'd take him away and I'd never see him again 'cause nobody likes a mean kid like me. That's what he said.'

Sara squatted down to get to his eye level. 'If he told you that he told you a lie, Jackie. And you're not a mean kid. And even if you are, I like you anyway. Who told you that lie?'

'He did. But I think he lies a lot. You're not really a grown-up at all, are you?'

'Why is that, Jackie?'

'Well, you're not very big, and you haven't yelled at me, even when I bit you. Grown-ups like to yell at people. Sometimes they like to hurt people, too. Come on, I'll show you the kitchen.' He led her through the swinging door into a large well-lighted country kitchen. The walls were lined with shelves, while across the room under the sunny windows she could see a dishwasher, gas stove, refrigerator, and freezer. A huge preparation counter took up one end of the room. A homey kitchen table sat in the middle of the floor.

'Take a pew,' Mrs Emory called out. 'Eggs and ham are ready, coffee's brewing, and bacon and toast to follow. Did you and Jack get along all right?'

'We got along fine,' Sara told her. 'After he gets to know my dog better I think we'll be good friends. But I can't eat all this for lunch! I have to watch my weight.'

'You have to learn the language out here in farm country,' Mrs Emory called. 'We eat a working breakfast at seven, we have dinner at noon, and we eat supper at six, when the workday is over. This is dinner. If you want lunch you have to go down to Amherst to the Lord Jeoffrey Hotel. There they serve lunch. Here we have dinner. And John said we have to fatten you up.'

'But I don't need fattening up,' Sara groaned. 'It took a long time to get me as thin as I am!'

Mrs Emory turned around from the stove to examine Sara more closely. She started to go back to her work, and then, struck by some thought, walked over to Sara and clutched a handful of her dress at the waistline. Immediately, under the pressure, the fully rounded curve of her hips appeared, and her breasts poked provocatively against the fabric. 'No,' Mrs Emory said shrewdly, 'there's more to you than meets the eye, Sara, isn't there?'

'He saw me on the beach, in all my old clothes,' Sara replied. 'He thinks I'm sweet sixteen and scrawny. I told him three times that he was wrong, but he didn't pay any attention.'

'Men don't when they've made up their minds,' Mrs Emory commented. 'And what about the baby?'

'Oh, the baby is real enough. I've been minding Pudge for three weeks. His mother had to have an eye operation—Sylvia, that's my brother's wife. Ralph came for Pudge this morning.'

'And all that other stuff—is he wrong there too?'

Sara shrugged her shoulders in dismay. 'He'd already made up his mind. I just couldn't seem to explain anything to him. I know he's a nice man, and I like him very much, but he's also a pompous, arrogant, chauvinistic——'

'Jackass,' Mrs Emory ended the sentence for her. 'I've been here since John was six years old, and everything you say is true. I'm glad you like him a lot. So do I. Now, dish up some of those eggs,' she instructed. 'You've had a hard day already, I can see. You can start dieting tomorrow, or some day soon.'

'Are you talking about Daddy?' the boy interrupted. 'Does Daddy diet? What does that mean, Sara?'

'It means not eating, so that you don't get too fat and then none of your clothes fit you,' Sara chuckled. 'And I suspect your father never diets, Jack. Come on, share some of these eggs. And could I have a plate for Mary, Mrs Emory? She likes eggs too, especially scrambled, but she won't eat if she doesn't have a plate of her own.'

'Is your dog going to be a problem, Sara?' asked the housekeeper as she passed over an empty plate. 'Will she stay in the kitchen? Or out in the barn?'

Sara pushed a generous portion of eggs and ham on to the plate and set it down on the floor in front of Mary. The big dog stood attentively in front of the plate, eyes on Sara. 'I guess if that's what people expect,

Mrs Emory, then Mary's going to be a problem,' Sara answered. 'Mary lives with me. She goes everywhere with me. She eats with me, she sleeps with me, and she even goes to the bathroom with me. I've had to live alone for some time, Mrs Emory. Mary is my guard dog, not my pet.'

'Why doesn't she eat the food, Sara?' Jackie interrupted.

'Oops! I forgot,' Sara returned. 'She's trained not to eat anything provided by anybody until I tell her to. Sometimes there are mean people who try to hurt guard dogs by poisoning them. If we all walked out of the room and left Mary here until tomorrow morning she still wouldn't touch the food. Now, watch!' She raised her right index finger and dropped it downward. 'Eat, Mary,' she said. The dog dived at the dish as if it were her first full meal since puppyhood.

'She acts on voice command, but also on hand signals, Jack. How's that for training.'

'That's marvellous,' Mrs Emory said. 'I wish some of our farm dogs could be half that well trained.'

'And she eats people who hurt Sara,' interjected the boy. 'Wait until Uncle Robert comes—I wanna see that!'

'Not to worry, then, Sara,' the housekeeper assured her. 'Now I understand the problem. We'll treat her like a seeing-eye dog. Does she really bite?'

'Everyone but kissing cousins!' Sara looked up and smiled as John came through the door. His face was lined with worry furrows, but he erased them quickly, patted the boy on the head, and sat down at the table.

'I'm sorry, Sara,' he apologised, 'I just can't seem to get my act completely lined up. That was Robert on the phone—my brother Robert. You'll see him tonight, by the way. He tells me that the grapevine says there'll be a strike at the plant on Monday. It seems that the union is just waiting for another incident. Now, everybody, eat up!'

Twenty minutes later he had cleaned his plate. Sara

was still wrestling with her coffee, and Jackie had slid out of his seat and was dancing up and down by the door.

'Now, Jack,' his father ordered, 'you take Sara up and show her her room. Get a little rest, Sara, have a hot bath. One thing we always have plenty of is hot water. Unpack when you want to—we've nothing else scheduled for today. And I'm glad to see that you and Jackie are getting along so well together.'

Sara stood up, but took one more swallow of coffee before she went. 'Thanks, Mrs Emory,' she called. 'Fine coffee. Better than I can make!'

'You're welcome, child,' the housekeeper replied. 'We'll get on better if you'll call me Emma,' she added.

Sara smiled and amended her statement. 'Thanks, Emma. I'll come and help clean up, if I may.'

'You'll do no such thing,' said John. 'You get yourself upstairs, get a bath, and rest this afternoon. Tomorrow I want you to come with me, and we'll go over to the Clinic. I want you to have a complete physical check-up.'

'Yes, master,' Sara mouthed at his broad back, and walked out of the kitchen. Jackie was waiting for her, impatiently tapping his foot on the bottom stair. He stretched out a hand to her and led her upstairs. The stairs curved gently, the heavy carpeting smothering any noises the two might have made. At the top landing they turned left and stopped at the second door. Jackie opened it and waved her in.

'You have the guest room, Sara,' he announced proudly. 'There's a bathroom over here, but you have to share it with me. That's my room, through that door.'

Sara was so absorbed in the beauty of the well-lit room that she gave the conversation little thought. 'Isn't that nice?' she murmured, looking at the view from the double windows. The entire room was decorated in light yellow and white, and the sun splashed through the windows like an engulfing sea. The furniture was sparse, but well built. A queen-sized bed dominated, covered by a gold bedspread. Her bags rested on the gold carpet at the foot of the bed.

'It's beautiful, Jackie,' she finally commented. 'But I do need a bath, and a rest—and us girls need a little privacy, so scoot out of here, young man! I'm glad we're going to be friends.'

He gave her a cheerful smile, and closed the door behind him. Sara took one more look around, gave a whoop of joy, pirouetted, and fell back on the bed. She clasped her hands behind her head and congratulated herself. John, John, John, she chortled to herself. Pompous, chauvinistic, tall. Homely, sexy, wonderful. John!

She closed her eyes, and John appeared before her. He reached out those wonderful arms towards her. He had two little horns growing out of the sides of his head, and a forked tail that lashed from side to side. He looked just exactly like Faust's Mephistopheles, and he would surely give any sensible girl a great deal of trouble. And that is just what I am looking for, isn't it? she asked herself. A great deal of trouble! Sara giggled at herself, and got up to unpack.

She hung up her new dresses in the cedar wardrobe without a great deal of enthusiasm. They looked lonely. When she added her few skirts and slacks, it still did not seem to cut down the loneliness at all. She started to add her uniform to the tiny row, then thought otherwise, this room certainly would not be as private as one might desire. So she put it back into the suitcase and stowed the case as far back as she could in the wardrobe. Her pile of nightgowns, dressing gowns, and filmy underwear she crammed into the capacious drawers of the big chest that stood against the wall. And only then did she investigate the rest of her new domain.

She opened one of the windows, and was inundated by the cloying sweetness of lilacs in full bloom. In the oak tree just outside the window a pair of chickadees chided each other as they worked on their nest. Sara smiled happily at them, then skipped into the bathroom. The bath was tiled in gold and green, matching the décor of her room. Thankfully she stripped off her travel clothes and dropped them into the big hamper that stood against the wall. The water ran hot and full. She filled the tub waist-deep, slurping in generous amounts of someone's bath powders. When she climbed into the warm relaxation of the water she gave a sigh of relief. She lay still for a while, then sat up and began soaping herself. It was then that she heard a movement behind her in the bedroom.

'Who's there!' she called.

'It's only me, Sara,' John answered. 'You went off so quickly that Mary couldn't get out of the kitchen door, so I brought her upstairs.'

'Thank you,' Sara called. 'Just turn her loose. I'm glad you two are getting along so well.'

His voice was louder, nearer. 'It's no problem,' he said.

Sara looked over her shoulder to see him standing in the doorway of the bathroom. She squeaked in surprise, her tiny hands reaching up automatically to unsuccessfully cover her full breasts. Then she sank down thankfully into the suds that covered the water, until only her head was visible.

'Want me to wash your back?' he asked.

'Well, really, Mr Englewood!' she spluttered.

'Yes, of course,' he replied. There was a sarcastic edge in his voice. 'Of course—I'd forgotten you're not as young as I thought. That is the phrase, isn't it?' And with that he walked out of the bathroom. A second later she heard the bedroom door slam shut behind him.

Mary came over and hung her head over the side of the tub.

'And what kind of a guard dog are you?' Sara muttered. But the melancholy look on the dog's face was more than she could take. She broke into laughter, threw her wet arms around the dog's neck, and hugged her tightly. 'Now for goodness' sake,' she admonished, 'stick close to me. I seem to be far at sea with a crew of loonies Stick close, dog!'

By the time she had dried herself thoroughly Sara's normally sunny disposition had returned. She slipped into her old green kimono and went to the window. She was looking south, down the river valley. Directly to the south, and across the river, the land was flat, with a strange whiteness about it. In the distance to the west she could see the looming hills of the Berkshires, but a haze left their peaks undefined. To the east she could see the line of trees that outlined the river, and beyond the river, among the sheltered hills, masses of apple orchards stood sentinel. She sat by the open window brushing her hair, at peace with her world.

Take a rest, everybody had said. So why not? She walked over to the bed and settled herself in its soft luxury. Her hair was still damp. She fluffed it out across the pillows to dry, and then closed her eyes. One hand dropped off the edge of the bed and fell on Mary's silky hair. The two communed quietly by touch, then together they drifted off to sleep.

A light rap on the door recalled Sara to the present. She had been having a wonderful dream. John had been hanging in chains before her while she, dressed in her skimpiest bikini, had been dancing around him, snipping off parts of his dark pinstriped suit with a pair of nail scissors. What it meant, she had no idea, but it had been thoroughly enjoyable. The knock was repeated. Unwilling to get up, she called, and the door opened. Jackie walked in, looked behind him carefully, and put a finger to his lips. He closed the door softly behind him.

'I'm resting too, Sara,' he whispered. 'Can I talk to you?'

'Of course, Jack. Sit here on the bed. Talk away.'

'If you didn't come to take my daddy away, why did you come, Sara?'

'I don't really know why, Jackie. Your Aunt Cindy

wanted me to come. And your daddy asked me to come. So here I am.'

'Uncle Robert was talking to Daddy in the library. He was laughing. They were talking about you. I don't like it when Uncle Robert laughs.'

'And you were snooping?'

'If I didn't snoop I'd never learn nothing around here. Nobody tells me nothing. It's always "Go away, Jackie. This isn't for little ears." Baloney! But that's not what I came for.'

'It's not? What did you come for?'

The boy sat down on the edge of the bed, and ran his hand through his hair, in almost the identical movement of his father when under stress. 'Do you like kids, Sara?' he asked.

'Yes, of course I do,' Sara laughed. 'My brothers have kids. I like them a lot.'

The boy sighed in relief. 'My father said you was coming to have a long rest, so I guess you wouldn't be too busy or nothing?'

'I suspect I might not be too busy. Too busy for what?'

'Sara, please don't be mad, but would you mind working for me?'

'You want me to work for you? Is this an offer of a steady paying job?' She suppressed the smile that would have accompanied the comment. The boy was too serious for joking.

'Part-time work,' he responded. 'I could pay you. I get an allowance—fifty cents a week.'

'Well, so far so good. What kind of work is it we're bargaining about?'

Jack hesitated, then committed himself, talking as fast as he could form the words. 'What I want you to do is to be my mother at the school. It's a Regional school, and all the other guys who don't come on the bus have their mother drive them, except I don't have no mother, and then they make fun of me and I get in a lot of fights, and I don't win any of them 'cause I'm too small, and I'm tired of getting beat up and sent home from school. Please?'

'You mean all I have to do is to drive you to school in the morning and look like a mother?'

'Yes, but—but you have to come for me after school, and—and you have to say all those mother things, like, you know, don't get your clothes dirty, or be a good boy, or like that. And then you——'

'And then I what? This sounds like the hard part.'

'And—well, then you—you have to kiss me. You know!'

'Ah!' Sara exclaimed. 'The monkey in the woodpile, huh? I have to kiss you every school day? And in front of the whole school? Are we going to be that good friends?'

'It's only acting, you know,' he explained seriously. 'You don't have to like it. It's just for show. And besides, you'll get paid for it.'

'Well, there's that.' She patted the pillow beside her. With a grateful sigh he shifted and lay down beside her. 'Could you?' he pressed.

'It would be a new business for me,' Sara reflected. 'I don't have any experience. I've never played Rent-a-Mother before—it's a pretty big job. It wouldn't be too much if it wasn't for that kissing stuff. Well, all right, I'll do it. But we'll have to ask your father, you know. I don't have a car. If he agrees, you've got a deal. Shake?'

Solemnly Jack extended a hand. 'But I couldn't let it go for less than five cents a week,' she added. 'Can you meet my terms?'

'Yeah, I guess I could afford that.' Then a moment of silence. 'Are you gonna rest some more, Sara?'

'I think so. Mary is still sleepy, so I guess I might rest some more.'

'Could I rest here with you, Sara? No kissing or no mush stuff, just resting. Could I?'

'Yup.' Five minutes of silence followed. Sara had almost fallen asleep again when she felt the hard little head butt into her shoulder. Cautiously she slipped an arm under him and pulled his head on to her breast. A little smile played around the corners of his mouth, and Jack wiggled closer, like a little puppy.

From somewhere in the distance she could hear a clock striking in a distant church tower, playing counterpoint to the bird songs outside the window. Mary grunted once or twice, and then all was quiet.

CHAPTER FOUR

IT was after five o'clock when Sara woke up. Somewhere in the distance she could hear that same clock striking, and a siren warbled. She stirred, trying to flex the stiff muscles in her right arm. The movement awakened both the child and the dog. Mary grumpily elevated herself to her four feet, then rested her head on the bed. The boy squirmed and rolled over so that his head rested on Sara's stomach. He opened both eyes wide and smiled at her. She sat up, ran her fingers through his soft hair, and returned the smile. There was a knock at the door, and Mrs Emory came in.

'Have you seen——' she started to say, then scanned the bed and laughed. She went back to the door. 'He's up here,' she shouted to someone. 'He's up here resting with Sara!' She came back into the room and shut the door behind her. 'And this will set the cat among the pigeons, my girl!' Sara tilted her head up and looked the question.

'The young man has been in a terrible temper for three days,' Mrs Emory explained. 'A real touch-me-not. Even his father could do little with him. And then today he went off to school and they sent him right back for fighting in the schoolyard. So the family has been afraid he'd do something stupid, like running away, perhaps. And him being missing for two hours, his father figured that this was the day. John was just about to call the police. Well, supper's ready in half an hour. Come on, you two.'

Sara looked down at the boy, fascinated by the intensity in his pleading eyes. 'Fighting in the schoolyard, eh?' she queried.

'Well, I told you,' the boy said. 'And if you go with me there won't be any more fights, 'cause I'll have a mom prettier than *any* of them.'

'Flattery will get you everywhere,' she retorted. She reached down a finger and tickled him under his ribs, and he rolled away, laughing. Mary gave a disapproving whine. 'Maybe we'd better get some practice in on this mother business. Monday isn't too far away. Let's give it a try right now?'

'Well-maybe,' he laughed. 'A little hug? I ain't ready for no kissing just yet.' Sara held out her arms. He stood up on the bed, bounced a couple of times as if on a trampoline, and dived at her. She squeezed him gently, then kissed his ear. 'That doesn't count,' she whispered, 'I'm just practising my aim!' They were both giggling as Sara swung him to the floor and followed suit. They went down the stairs together, Sara in the middle, Mary padding on her left, and Jack holding her hand on the right. John was standing at the foot of the stairs a puzzled frown on his face.

He swung his son up into his arms for a quick hug, set him back down on the floor, and pointed him towards the rear of the house. 'Wash your face,' he commanded. When the boy had disappeared he looked back to Sara.

'More magic, Sara?' he asked.

She stopped in front of him, hands clasped behind her back. She wanted desperately to make some clever remark, but her mind had turned to jelly. 'What?' she asked feebly.

'Magic,' he repeated. 'Or is it witchcraft? First it was Aunt Lucinda, now it's Jackie. And I've lived in this house for twenty-seven years with Mrs Emory and never knew that her name was Emma. And it only took you two hours. Magic?'

Sara remained still, tongue-tied, then she lowered her head, unwilling to meet the gleam in his eye. Try as she might she could find no ready retort. She shrugged her shoulders.

'Or is it that Sara Anderson is just a very likeable person? Another time we must discuss this further. My brother is here for just a few minutes,' he added. 'He won't stay to supper, but he wants to meet you.'

'But my hair—I need to———'

'Later, Sara, later.' He led her by the hand through the double doors to the left of the main entrance, into a room which was both sitting room and office. She made a few ineffectual motions at smoothing the creases in her dress, then was propelled forward by John's hand at her back. The only occupant of the room, leaning with an arm on the mantel over the fireplace, smiled at her. Sara gasped. He was taller than John by a couple of inches, broader of shoulder, and blond where John was dark. His face was unmarked, smooth. He looked the very picture of Michelangelo's David. He wore a gold sports coat over a white turtleneck sweater. His sleekly tailored slacks clung tightly to well-muscled thighs and legs. Compared to him John looked slight, craggy, and dark.

Sara took six steps into the room and halted. The man uncoiled himself from the mantelpiece and stalked across the room, smiling down at her through brilliant blue eyes. He extended a hand for one of hers, but Sara backed away, bumping into Mary's nose. She folded both hands behind her and looked him over.

'So this is little Sara,' the giant said. His voice was a fine-tuned tenor, and he played it knowledgeably. 'Welcome to Deerfield, little Sara. Would you like a Coke before dinner?'

'No, thank you,' she offered primly, biting back the notion to ask him to add a couple of shots of Bacardi to it. He made a little face. 'Now then,' he said, 'let's have a good look at you!' He grabbed her by both shoulders, lifted her up off her feet, and turned her so that the light of the chandelier struck full on her face. Sara spluttered at him, while Mary growled deeply, reared up on her hind legs, and seized one of his wrists in her capacious mouth. The dog's hold was firm, and not too gentle.

'My God!' he roared. 'Somebody get this damn animal off of me! Help me, John!'

'I think,' Sara gasped, 'if you'd stand still and put me down? There's a good boy. That's better.' She stepped away from him, rubbing her shoulders. 'Down, Mary. Guard!' she commanded. The dog released the wrist, but stood stiff-legged, mouth half open, both eyes glued on Robert. Sara backed away from him, only to find that she had backed directly into John's arms. Mary looked, approved, and returned to her guard station.

'Would somebody explain to me what's going on?' Robert asked in an aggrieved tone. He rubbed his wrist, trying to restore the circulation.

'Mary is my guard dog,' Sara explained. 'She's trained to protect me. I don't allow people to put their hands on me. And what I don't like, Mary doesn't like either.'

'Of course, Sara,' Robert said smoothly. 'I was only taking an avuncular interest, you know. You and I have a lot in common, Sara. We'll have to get together and talk some time soon.

He also had one thing in common with his brother, Sara thought. His voice was hypnotic, and he knew how to use it. Almost she could believe that she liked him—almost. She studied him carefully. There was no denying his charm, his good looks, his boyish smile. But then it struck her—his smile. He smiled with full lips, strong teeth, dimpled cheek. But the smile never reached his eyes.

He was looking her over too, she knew. A tiny thing, no figure to speak of, a poorly-fitted dress. Disarranged straw-coloured hair, hanging below her shoulders. A kid—and hardly a tempting kid. Her only conceivable asset was fifteen per cent of the stock of Englewood Industries. His smile turned off. Sara could almost hear the switch click.

'John? What about it? You and I have over eighty per cent of the voting shares. Shall we cancel the dividend?'

'I don't know, Robert. If we do that will make it five times in the past two years. You're sure we must?'

'There are the figures, John.' Robert gestured to some printed pamphlets lying on the coffee table next to the sofa. 'We haven't made a profit in over a year. Sales are up. Expenses are up. Profits are down. Read it and weep.'

John pushed a tired hand up through his hair and sighed. 'You know I don't understand that Corporate gibberish, Robert. Sometimes I think you hire a man especially to write and confuse people. Well, if you must. But we can't keep on this way much longer. And don't forget that Sara has a voting and an income interest in this, too.'

'Then I take it we're agreed,' said Robert. 'Well, I've got to be on my way—I have a heavy date in Amherst tonight, and I may stay for the weekend. See you!' He walked out of the room. John followed him to the front door, Sara close on his heels.

'Got a new car?' John called after him. Robert turned and waved acknowledgment as he slipped into the gull-wing door of the sports car.

'Nice car,' John said absently to Sara as he closed the door. 'Wonder what kind it is. Robert has a thing about cars.'

'Delorian,' muttered Sara. She had a thing about cars, too, but not the income to support it. 'Retails at twenty-five thousand dollars per copy.'

'You must be mistaken, Sara,' John chuckled. 'We none of us have that kind of money this year. Robert is putting everything he's got into the factory. Come on, let's have supper.'

As they walked back down the hall towards the dining room Jackie stuck his head out from behind the stairs. 'Has he gone?' he asked. 'Uncle Robert—has he gone?'

'Yes, he's gone, son. You should have come out to meet him.'

Very slowly, stubbornly, the little boy shook his head in disagreement, then followed them both in for supper.

After supper John excused himself, and took a stack

of college papers into the sitting room with him. Sara joined Mrs Emory in the kitchen, helping to stack and rinse the dishes. At eight o'clock, when the work was done, and Mrs Emory had retired to her own private suite at the far end of the house, Sara snatched Jackie out from in front of the twenty-five-inch colour TV set, ran him through a quick bath, then tucked him in for the night.

'Leave the door open, Sara,' he pleaded. 'I might need you in the dark. Please?'

'Promise,' she said. She sat with him until he had fallen asleep, and then, for want of something better to do, she dug out her sewing bag and wandered downstairs again. After sunset things had cooled considerably, and the central heating system had not been turned on as yet. When she saw the flames flickering in the fireplace in the sitting room she smiled and walked in. John, who had been hidden from her by the high wing-back chair before the fireplace, squirmed around to look over his shoulder as he heard her.

'Most comfortable in front of the fire, Sara,' he called. 'Pull a chair over here.'

'I'd prefer this, if you don't mind, John.' She picked up one of the several large floor pillows that were scattered around the room. Then with bag and pillow in hand she walked over to his chair, plunked the pillow down at his feet, and gracefully coiled herself up on it.

'This is lovely,' she told him as she felt the first wave of heat from the fireplace. She wriggled a bit to get herself settled, arched her neck, and combed her hair forward over her shoulders into the projected warmth. 'Beats TV a mile, doesn't it?'

He agreed with her. 'We have a wonderful cable TV system here in the valley. It gives us thirty-six channels of service, but not a programme worth watching.'

'Will I bother you if I work here, John?' she asked.

'No, not at all. I'm reading this young man's proposal for his thesis,' he added. 'This makes the third time I've read it. I'm so sleepy I can hardly keep my eyes open, but I promised him a report tomorrow morning at the latest, so I must read, and comment, before I can get to bed. Mrs Emory has promised to read him my comments by telephone tomorrow morning.'

'You didn't get any more sleep last night, then?' Sara pulled the collapsible frame out of her bag, locked in the pattern, and began to work as she talked.

'Oh, perhaps four hours last night. What's that you're making?'

'It's a cover for a footstool, for Ralph. I'm making it in gros-point. You remember about Ralph and Sylvia?'

'Oh, him—Pudge's father. And Sylvia is his wife. And you make things for them?'

'Sure. I'm very fond of Ralph. And Sylvia too, of course.'

'It must be very heavy work,' he commented. 'That looks like burlap that you're working on.'

'You're altogether too clever—for a man!' she laughed. 'It is burlap. Most people use a heavy reinforced plastic, but I prefer the old ways. It's Scorpio I'm doing—that's Pudge's birth sign.'

Both worked in companionable silence for a time, until the telephone rang. John picked up the extension and listened. He asked a quiet question, then hung up. Sara turned around to face him, resting her elbows on his knee. 'More trouble?' she asked.

'I don't know,' he replied. 'It was Western Union—a telegraph message for you.' He checked a pencilled note on his pad. 'It came from Dallas Texas. It says "Call me within twenty-four hours or I will come to get you. Signed David." Sara?'

'Ooh, that man!' she groaned in fury.

'David?'

'No, Ralph. I told Ralph I was coming. It was all so simple. He threatened he'd call David! Damn!'

'Okay now, because I forgot. Which one is David?'

'My brother—my big brother David. He's the youngest of the boys. I told you he worked in Dallas.'

'So?'

'So for some reason they all think that David knows how to handle "sweet little Sara" when she gets some harebrained idea. I'd better call him. If I don't he will.'

'Will what?'

'He'll come up here and blow your house down!'

'He'd have to be pretty big to do that,' commented John.

'He's big enough. May I call him?'

He handed her the telephone and watched as she dialled the number she knew so well. When the telephone had been answered at the other end she said, 'It's Sara!' and then held the instrument away from her ear. There was a stream of loud noise from the phone. When it stopped she put the instrument to her ear and said quickly, 'It's only a case, David—honestly. Ralph has it all mixed up. I'm here on a case. There's a little boy with a serious problem, and I—yes, I know, David. I admit I'm a sucker for a sob story, but it's really a case. He's a nice little boy and I like it up here, and if you *dare* to do that, David Anderson, I shall cry, and you know you can't stand that! Mr Englewood is such a—put him on? Well, all right, David, but you watch your language. He's a college professor, and the father of the boy.' She handed the phone back to John.

He introduced himself, then sat back and listened for three minutes a series of ridiculous expressions running across his face. Then, looking grim, he said, 'Yes,' and hung up.

'Your brother tells me you're very precious, and much younger than you appear, and *he* was not prepared to worry about your health or your virtue, and if *I* didn't he would personally come up here and break both my legs. He sounded very—positive?'

'Yes,' she said glumly. 'That's the trouble. He means it all. He doesn't know beans about women either. All the other boys know that I always do what he tells me to do. But that's only because I always get him to tell me what I really want to do in the first place. Does that sound ever so complicated?'

'No. I think vaguely that I understand. Doesn't sound like a nice sort of brother to have.'

'He's nice to me, John,' she explained. 'Not to anybody else. He works in a very physical trade down there. He's part of a large group of very—forceful people.'

'What kind of work does he do?'

'I can't explain it clearly, John. They call him the Enforcer.'

'Sounds pretty fierce.' He was speaking solemnly, but there was a hard glint in his eye. Or perhaps it was the flickering light from the fireplace? 'What do the rest of them do, Sara?'

Sara studied him. It had not seemed to be a casual question. She finally decided to answer, but with reservations. 'Well, of course you know Ralph,' she said. 'He works in Boston. He's in the numbers business. And Jim—he's the one in California—he works in drugs and things. And I told you about David.'

John threw up both his hands 'Okay, Sara,' he said. 'I give up. I get the message. Play nice with Sara or Big Brother will get you! Well, at least I've finished this report.' He thumped the mass of paper down on the table and laid his pencilled notes across their top. 'And now I think it's time for me to get to bed. Sleep late if you want to, Sara. But about ten o'clock I want you to go with me to the clinic for a complete physical.' He snapped off the table lamp beside his chair and leaned forward to run his fingers through her hair. 'Pure silk,' he marvelled. 'And the softness of your skin, Sara!' His fingers slid down on to her cheek and traced a circle around to the back of her neck. 'Mary doesn't care?'

Sara looked over at her valiant protector, fast asleep on the braided rug in front of the fireplace. 'Mary doesn't care if I don't,' she said. Silently they both stood up. John took her hand and they walked to the stairs together. Not until they reached the door did Mary gather her bones together and get up to follow them.

Alone in her bedroom, Sara left the lights off while she looked out at the sparkling countryside. He'll never change his opinion, she told herself. He still thinks I'm a—and now he thinks my family is a bunch of gangsters, or something. And yet he touches me. Why? Well, I don't care! But of course she did. She snapped the shades down, almost ripping them off in her anger and disgust. Then she turned on a table lamp and thumbed through her wardrobe for her favourite nightgown. 'So it's only a fantasy,' she snarled at Mary. 'At least it will make me feel better!' She looked in on Jackie as she went into the bathroom for a shower. The boy had not stirred, but his covers were off. She replaced them, took her shower, and gently slid the nightgown over her head.

'If your mother could see you now, Susan Antonia,' she chided herself as she stood before the full-length mirror in the bedroom. Nightgowns had always been her passion—frilly, fantastic, useless things that she could wear in the privacy of the night; things that prim and respectable Sara would never consider in the daytime, brought joy to Susan Antonia in the night. And this one was the most useless of them all. It was a white silk transparent veil, nothing more, hugging her hips tightly before it fell away to an ankle-length swirl. The bodice consisted of two separate panels that covered her breasts, but concealed nothing. They were held up by two shoestring straps that crossed in the middle of her bare back and then daintly merged into the fabric again at her hips.

'Sensuous Sara?' she lectured her mirror reflection. 'Sexy Sara?' hopefully. 'Stupid Sara!' she concluded, then stuck her tongue out at her image, and dived into bed. In minutes she was asleep, bothered by no dreams at all.

When the noise wakened her she came back to the

world grumpily. Her wrist watch said one o'clock in the morning. She listened more carefully. The noise had risen in tone and pitch, a mewling, whining sound, like an animal in pain. Sara slid out of bed, fumbling for her slippers on the cold floor. Finding neither slippers nor robe in the darkness, she hurried towards the bathroom. By the time she reached the door the sound had become a scream, vibrating off the solid old walls in waves of pain and echo. Sara bolted into Jackie's room.

The little boy was sitting huddled in the far corner of his bed. His eyes were awash with tears, his mouth gobbled for breath as he screamed. 'Mommy! Mommy!' he yelled. 'Don't leave me, Mommy! Don't let him take you away!'

Sara vaulted across the bed and caught his tiny body up against her, burying his screaming, squirming form against the softness of her breasts. The screams continued, but gradually dropped in force, until at last he lay loosely against her, sobbing uncontrollably. Sara crooned meaningless sounds at him, stroked his hair, and held on. A separate noise caught her attention, and she looked up and saw John standing just inside the bedroom door.

The boy continued to sob. 'Mommy, don't leave me. Mamma? Mamma?' He squirmed up against Sara now, burrowing into her softness.

'I won't leave you, Jackie,' she soothed. 'Everything will be all right. Sara is here, and Daddy is here, and there's nothing to be worried about.' Softly she began to sing a lullaby in her low clear voice. Gradually the tears slowed, and then stopped. The little head remained burrowed into her, but his breathing was sweet and regular. Jack had fallen asleep again. His father came over to the bed, lifted him from Sara's arms, and tucked him back into bed. The two adults watched for a while, then Sara beckoned John into her room. She half closed the door behind her, and snapped on a light.

'I think I'd better sit up for a while,' she whispered, 'in case there's another outbreak. Does he do this often?'

'I'll stay a while, too, Sara,' he said tiredly. He sank gratefully into the upholstered chair that was placed at the head of her bed. 'It's pretty regular. Since his mother died, that is. I didn't want to get you involved in it, Sara.'

He was sitting forward, elbows on knees staring disconsolately into the darkness. She walked over and ruffled his hair. 'I want to get involved, John. I've a lot of experience with this sort of thing, and I want to help.'

'Do you, Sara? It really is Sara the Nice, isn't it?' His voice was fading slightly.

'But what he said, John. Who was it?'

'Who was what?'

'Who was it that was taking her away?'

But the only answer she got was a burble of air through his slightly opened mouth. He had made the fatal mistake of leaning back against the soft padding of the chair, and was instantly claimed by the sleep which he had been dodging for almost thirty-six hours.

'I can't leave you there,' Sara scolded him softly. 'You'll wake up with a sore neck and a terrible disposition!' She estimated his weight, and walked out into the hall to look in on his bedroom. It was too far away for her to carry or guide him to it. With a sigh of disgust at her own missed sleep she went back to him. She removed his slippers, slid him out of his robe, and then, using her nursing experience, managed to half carry, half urge him into her bed. It was not until she had him tucked in, dead to the world, that it struck her that he had worn nothing under the robe!

She laughed ruefully as she watched him, warm and snug in her own bed, while she stood in the middle of the room, shivering in the night cold. She walked up and down the room several times, rubbing her shoulders for warmth. She peeped in on Jackie, thinking perhaps to share his bed, but the boy had managed to sprawl completely across the middle of his narrow cot. Slowly Sara wandered back into her own room. 'He's in your bed, you can go to his,' she told herself, but it was a losing argument, for deep inside her head an insistent voice was saying, 'Be a devil, Sara. He can't do you out of your own bed. Be a devil, Sara!' And she was.

Trying carefully not to wake him, she went around to the other side of the bed, folded back the covers, and climbed in. At first she held herself firmly to her side of the bed, one hand actually clenching the mattress, but the coolness of the sheets, or the pitch of the mattress towards the centre, or that insistent voice in her head, finally broke her hold, and she slid inexorably into the warmth and comfort of John's touch. 'In for a penny, Sara,' she told herself, and cuddled up against him, her soft hair spreading across his right arm as he slept. She turned on her side, facing him, and gently moved her right hand up on to his chest, trying to make her breathing conform to his, trying to keep from squeaking at the thrill that contact made. Little images of "what if" ran through her mind, until, much against her will, Sara too was overcome by the events of the day and dived into sleep.

Once, later in the night, she awoke with a start, not knowing where she was, or what had disturbed her. And then she noticed that their positions were changed. She was now lying flat on her back, and John had turned on his side towards her. His left hand was responsible—it had come to rest on the generous curve of her hip, and then had marched slowly across her hip to her stomach, leaving a trail of fire behind it. It halted for a moment, tracing little circles of delight where his fingers slipped off the nightgown on to her skin. Gradually the hand moved up, until it completely cupped her left breast. He mumbled in his sleep at that point, and the hand gently squeezed, then moved up to trap her swelling nipple between index and forefinger.

She relaxed to the joy of it, surprised that her breasts had so swiftly responded, revelling in the thrill that started deep in her stomach and ran up through her brain. She held her breath, waiting for his next move. When, after ten minutes, nothing else happened, she almost started to cry in frustration. 'Stupid Sara!' she reminded herself. 'He's so dead to the world you could be a dressmaker's mannequin. Or any woman.' Disgusted with herself, she tried to move away from him, but his arm would not allow it. She forced herself to lie still, and eventually fell asleep again.

On her next awakening the sun was shining brightly in her window. She sat up with a start, to find herself all alone in the middle of the bed. 'Sara, Sara, Sara,' she sighed, 'what have you come to? You went out of your way to seduce the man, and you wake up in an empty bed—and nothing happened! Or did it?'

There was more than just the coolness of the breeze that bothered her. She looked down at herself to find that both shoulder straps of her nightgown had fallen off her shoulders, and the flimsy creation was bunched around her waist, leaving her nude from that point upward. She shivered, not from the cold, but because she could not remember. If only he had, she thought, running her own hands up from her narrow waist and across her breasts, to rest on opposite shoulders. If only he had. And *then* what would David say? Resolutely she put the whole puzzle out of her mind, scrambled out of bed, and went to brush her teeth.

She was still daydreaming as she changed into her bikini briefs. It didn't seem worthwhile to choose a dress They were all the same, terrible. In such a short time she had come to hate those shifts. She closed her eyes and reached into the wardrobe, grabbing a dress at random. Then she squeezed her feet into sandals brushed and braided her hair, and tiptoed downstairs. No one else seemed to be stirring except Mary. After she reached the bottom of the stairs she heard a slight noise at the top, behind her. She shushed Mary and backed against the swinging door into the kitchen. Then she closed the door quietly in front of her and turned, to find herself pinioned in John's arms. She breathèd a sigh of relief and relaxed against him, wiggling her arms into a comfortable position around his waist. He pushed her away immediately.

'Sit down,' he commanded. 'Do you want coffee?'

'I'm not sure,' she said, totally confused. 'Would you mind sitting at the other end of the table?'

'Why? Is that the only way we're ever going to have a conversation? I want to sit here, next to you.' And he did.

Sara sat up straight, with her hands folded in her lap, as she tried to control the massive flow of feelings her several senses were pouring into her brain.

'Mr Englewood——' she started out.

'Since we spent the night in the same bed you'd better call me John!'

'Mr Englewood,' she said in an exasperated tone of voice, 'I'm a perfectly normal woman, somewhat noted for being sensible. I speak calmly to people, and I don't get excited, and some are nice enough to say that I'm reasonably intelligent. Except when you're around, Mr Englewood. And as for sleeping together in my bed, I couldn't let you stay in a chair, could I? And I couldn't carry you back to your own bed, could I? And I——'

'But you didn't have to climb into bed *with* me, Sara, did you?'

'No, but I——' She looked up into his face, searching for some clue as to his feelings, and what she saw turned her heart to stone. Without any doubt, it was disgust that was twisting at the corners of his mouth.

'I don't intend to be your judge, Sara, but I did ask you not to play those games around here. We've put your past behind us. I understand you better now, what with one of your brothers into drugs, the other in mob work, and your lover in numbers. And there's no use arguing with me. We both know what you've been, don't we?'

'No, we don't, John,' she answered softly. 'No, we don't. When you're ready to believe me I'll tell you all about it.'

'What's to tell? I bring you home. You're nice to everybody, from top to bottom. And on your first night here you crawl into bed with me. Don't try to explain it, Sara, but do cut it out! You didn't have to climb in bed with me, did you, Sara?'

'No,' she admitted, shaking her head at herself. 'No, I didn't have to do that. I don't know why I did it. Now, please may I have some coffee and change the subject, and—did you?'

'Did I what, Sara?'

'Did you do—anything? Like—you know. Did you?'

'Don't remember, Sara?'

'No,' she lied valiantly, 'I don't remember anything!'

'Then I didn't do anything, Sara.'

She gulped at her coffee, and almost choked on it. John reached over and covered her hand with his. 'But I learned one thing for sure, Sara. You certainly *are* older than I thought, and as soon as you've had your breakfast you can go back upstairs and take off this damn disguise!' He fingered the hem of her skirt and threw it back at her.

'And how do you know all that if you didn't——' she flared at him.

'Come on, Sara. You were parading around almost inside that nightgown you were wearing for an hour, with the lights on. I don't know why you wear it—it certainly won't keep you warm. Now, how old are you?'

'I'm—I'll be twenty-four in June,' she whispered. There was a very interesting spot on the floor. She studied it carefully. 'I told you the first time we met, then I told you again, but you never listened. You seemed to be——'

'Pompous,' he interjected. 'A fine well-rounded word. A judgmental word, of course. Mrs Emory mentioned it to me.'

Sara raised her head and looked angrily at him. 'And

well deserved, too!' She found it hard to keep the tears from her eyes. 'And when I said it to Emma she said "pompous jackass" and I wished I'd known that from the beginning, and I'm never going to talk to anybody around here again, because you're all a bunch of—how can a girl have any secrets when every time I tell somebody they immediately repeat them, and I wish you'd go away! I don't seem to be making much sense even to myself, and it only happens when you're around!' She banged her tiny fist on the table and managed to overturn both their coffee cups. She looked at the spreading mess, then jumped to her feet. 'Damn! Damn!' she bawled. She turned and ran to the kitchen door, but stopped and turned to face John. The tears were rolling down her face, and there was an expression of loss and defeat on her face, but she stuck to her guns.

'I'm going upstairs to pack my bags,' she told him. 'But tell me, Mr Sanctimonious Englewood. When you woke up this morning and found this—this hooker—in your bed, did you immediately run away from the abomination? Or did you touch her?'

His face, white and tight-lipped, and then suddenly red, told her without words. She stalked out of the kitchen and up to her room.

CHAPTER FIVE

THE knock on the door was followed by Emma's voice. 'Nine-thirty, Sara!' she called. 'John asked me to remind you that you're leaving at ten. Sara?'

'Okay, Emma,' she called, 'I'll be ready.'

She got up from the bed, stalked towards the bathroom, then stopped and came back to Mary, stretched out in the middle of the floor. 'And if I were in my right mind I'd pack up, bag and baggage. That's what he thinks I am—a baggage. Shouldn't I, Mary?'

The big dog followed her pacing with a turn of the head. 'And before I left I would give him a very large piece of my mind!' She savoured the idea, then stalked into the bathroom and splashed water on her face to eradicate the tears. 'And believe me, I could do it. You hear, Mary?' The dog got up and ambled into the bathroom behind her. 'And do you know why I don't, Mary? I don't because of that poor little kid. Imagine having only John Englewood for a relative! If it wasn't for Jackie I'd pack my bags and get out of this place in under a minute!' The dog whuffed and sat down on the bathroom rug. Sara reached blindly for a towel to dry her face, then knelt down in front of Mary and hugged her. 'I know I'm lying,' she whispered, 'and if you ever tell a soul you'll be back in the Army! I do so love him, Mary—I do so it aches. I thought loving would be fun, but instead I'm on a roller-coaster. Maybe I really hate him! How can you love a man who thinks that if he touches you he'll catch some loathsome disease? What am I going to do, Mary?'

The dog staunched a further flow of tears by beginning to systematically wash the girl's face, using that big rough tongue as a rasp. Sara endured it for two minutes then laughed and pushed the massive head away.

79

'Yes, there's always that,' she commented. 'But I'm not sure how he'd react if I tried to lick his face. C'mon, pup, leg's get dressed!'

Back in the bedroom she coiled her braids up into a coronet, pinned them carefully, then stepped into a mid-calf wrap around skirt, and topped it all off with a soft cotton blouse with a ruffled collar. She snapped Mary's harness in place, then took one last look at them both in the mirror. 'Well, we're both beautiful, Mary,' she commented. 'That will do something to build up my confidence. So off we go, Nanook!'

Twenty minutes later she was sitting in the front seat of the Chrysler LeBaron, with the sun-roof open. John came out of the house and joined her. Mary climbed around in the rear seat, and finally settled down. So far he had not said a word. When he reached for the ignition key Sara put her hand on his arm and stopped him.

'Are you very mad at me?' she asked.

'No, I'm not angry with you at all,' he said. 'I'm glad you decided not to go. Are you angry with me?'

'I can't decide,' she said honestly. 'One minute I hate you, and then in another minute I—I don't hate you. I'm very mixed up, John. But if you're not mad at me, I have another problem that requires your help.'

'Hmmm?' He started the engine, and spent a minute checking lights and dials.

'Jackie has asked me to do something for him,' she explained hurriedly. 'He wants me to drive him to and from school every day. But of course I would have to borrow a car.'

He looked at her and frowned. 'You don't have to do things like that, Sara,' he told her. 'You're not the hired help around here, you're one of the family. Frank usually drives him in.'

'But I'd like to do it,' she responded, looking straight ahead to avoid falling into the deep pools of his eyes. 'It's a problem of peer pressure, John. All the other kids are driven to school by their mothers. He wants a woman to——'

'Ah—he wants to have a big sister to drive him in?'

'Well, perhaps something like that,' she mumbled. 'He's offered to pay me, you know. Five cents a week. It's been a long time since I've had a steady job. May I?'

'No reason why not,' he laughed. 'A nickel a week? Not bad. I do suppose you have a licence? Or do you? We did establish that you were over sixteen, didn't we?'

'Really now,' she protested in some heat, 'I do have a licence. Do you want to——'

'No, you don't have to show it to me. By now they had come to the end of the gravel road that joined the farm to the paved highway. 'Watch to the right for me, Sara. This is a blind corner.' When they were safely out on the highway John continued, 'We have a VW bug in the garage. Elena used to drive it. I'll have Frank's mechanic check it out, and you can use that. And not just for driving Jackie to school, Sara. Use it for yourself, for whatever you want.'

They travelled the rest of the way in silence. Just before the centre of town John turned off the road and into a large paved parking lot. The building which fronted the parking area was a single-story white concrete structure with a flat roof, and no windows. It seemed to stretch for hundreds of yards in every direction.

'But there aren't any windows!' Sara exclaimed in surprise. 'All those people and no windows?'

'We employ about three hundred and fifty people,' he replied. 'There *are* windows, but only in the office area. The work we do is very sensitive to temperature, humidity, and dust. Every workroom is isolated, air-conditioned, and as dust-proof as we can make it.'

'What is it that you manufacture?' she probed.

'An electronic component, Sara. Integrated circuits. Chips, we call them. Here, look at this.' He pulled out of his pocket a tiny oblong piece of opaque plastic. 'Inside this little chip are all the circuits you need to build a radio receiver,' he told her. 'All you need to do is add power, an antenna, and a loudspeaker. We manufacture six types of ICs here. Other manufacturers use them in computers, games, TV sets, and military weapons. In fact, they're used in almost everything these days. There's a big demand for them. Every Tom, Dick, and Ivan is out to beg, buy, or steal them.'

'But you're not making a profit? That doesn't sound right.'

'*We* are not making a profit, Sara. We. You're in it too, don't forget. I don't know why. I am an engineer. I designed these circuits, and the machines we use to make them. But I'm not a businessman. That's Robert's field.'

'Robert is trained in management?'

'You'd bétter believe it!' He smiled as if proud of his only brother. 'Graduated with honours from Harvard School of Business Administration. Robert's the whiz-kid of the family. I'd like to show you around the plant, Sara,' he added, 'but it's Saturday, and all the lines are shut down for the weekend.'

'But if the plant is shut down, why did you bring me here?'

'The plant is shut down, but the doctor is a friend of mine. And Saturday is the best time for the clinic to handle an outside case. It's all just for you, Sara.'

'Just for me? That must cost a pretty penny. Can you just order something like that to happen?'

He set the handbrake and reached across her to open her door. Once again the touch of his arm against her breast startled her. She drew back from his touch. 'I don't give any orders in the plant,' he continued. 'Doctor Fineberg is an old friend. He's doing this as a favour.' He climbed out of the car, came around, and helped Sara and Mary out of the low seats. 'Now, you go in. They're waiting for you. I'll be back to pick you up.'

It was more than three hours later that Sara was finally returned to the little office where Doctor Fineberg waited for her.

'Tired?' he asked as he scanned the papers on his clipboard.

'Very much so,' she admitted, dropping into the proffered chair. 'That's the most thorough examination I've ever had. Your little clinic has more gadgets than the whole hospital where I last worked.'

'Ah,' he said absentmindedly. 'Our gynaecological exam does not seem at all in consonance with what your medical history would indicate. When did you last have a physical?'

'About eight months ago.'

'What brought about that exam?' he asked, his head bent over the form he was filling out.

'Oh, the usual staff exam,' she replied. 'Massachusetts General requires a full medical every six months for nursing staff.'

The doctor's head snapped up. 'You were on the nursing staff at Mass General? What position?'

'Night supervisor for the two pediatric words.'

'You must be a Registered Nurse? Why did you give it up?'

'My mother became terminally ill, so I went home to nurse her. She died about two months ago. I was just about to start out in private nursing when John—when Mr Englewood came for me.'

'Well,' said the doctor. He ran his eyes up and down the top sheet on the clipboard. 'That's very interesting. I have the feeling that my good friend John is in for some surprises any one of these days. He was the one who gave us the data for your initial medical record, you know.'

He stood up and stretched, a wrinkly chubby man with the end of a tiring week in sight. 'Of course it will be some time before we get all the lab reports back. If I can find a typist, we'll forward a full report. In the meantime, if you feel like putting in a few hours on occasion, we're always shorthanded.'

'Thank you, doctor,' she smiled, 'But I've already had the offer of one steady job, and I don't think I can take on a second one at this time. Perhaps later?'

He waved her out the door, chuckling because she looked so young, so desirable, so naïve. She smiled back at him, thinking of the contrast between the two jobs she had been offered. John was waiting for her in the car.

'What's so funny?' he asked as she climbed into the seat beside him.

'Oh, I don't know,' she chuckled. 'It seems that everything comes up in bunches. Yesterday I got the offer of a steady job from Jackie, and now Doctor Fineberg's made me another!'

'Don't take that sort of thing seriously, Sara,' he cautioned. 'You don't need a job up here. You're here to relax, to see how the other people live. Besides, Fineberg is too old for you.'

'I don't know why you say that,' Sara responded. She leaned over the seat and was scratching Mary's neck. Then, without thinking, 'They say that the older ones are a lot better than some of the young ones!'

'Do they indeed!' he snarled, and drove off like the wind. For the life of her Sara was unable to figure out why *he* should be angry. After all, she told herself, she was the one who ought to be angry about the day. 'And I am!' she confided to herself. 'And I'm going to tell him about it!'

When they pulled up beside the house there was another car already standing there. Sara inspected the bright red Ferrari sports car with more than casual interest. 'Damn!' John muttered. 'Robert's back. I didn't expect him back again this weekend—he has his own house down in Amherst. Damn!' Sara reached over for the door handle, and he stopped her.

'I thought we'd go have a sit-down in the parlour, and have a long talk. But with Robert here, that won't work. I need to talk to you.'

'And I need to talk to you,' Sara announced as coldly as she could manage. She turned towards him, shifting her left leg up on to the seat, careless of the lovely knee displayed. 'I've gone along with your little charade this morning, John. This "Sara must have a physical" thing is about as blatant as you could get. I don't lose my temper very often, but I'm as close to it now as you could wish for. What's the matter? Is Sara a pest-carrier? Did you expect me to infect your precious little family with bubonic plague, or leprosy, or some social disease?'

His face darkened under his tan, and he held off answering for a moment. 'I—to be honest with you——'

'Yes, let's do!' She stabbed him with each word. 'Let's be honest. I'm a little tired of all this Yankee rectitude.'

'Give me some credit, Sara! I was concerned about you. You lived at the beach, but your cheeks were pale and drawn. You've obviously been through a trying time. But—well, your occupation is a strange one, and I——'

'For the last time, John, I am not what you think. Are you afraid? Are you worried about VD? I suppose a big boy like you would realise that you catch that only by seduction, John. Is the idea too much for your delicate stomach? Well, all you have to do is make sure that you avoid that, isn't it? Here, touch my hand!' she snapped. 'I swear to you that even if I were overflowing with infection you can't get it by touching me. Go ahead, show me how much confidence you have in sweet little misguided Sara. Go ahead, touch me!' She held out her hand to him, daring him. He was grinding his teeth in rage.

He seized her wrist, pulled her across the seat, hard up against his steel frame. Then he wrapped one arm around her, and pushed her closer still, with one hand in the small of her back. With the other hand he tilted her chin up, then lowered his face to hers, and lightly caressed her lips with his. It was a gesture at first, but then he renewed the contact against her lips. Sara sighed surrender, and pressed herself closer to him as she opened her lips. The sweet pain of passion swept over her. For endless minutes she clung to him, and when he gently set her aside, she collapsed in her seat, a vision of total dejection. She pried her eyes open and looked at him.

He was sitting back in his seat, a strange disturbed look on his face. He fumbled for a cigarette, and when he lit it she could see that his hand was trembling.

'Sara?' His voice was raspy rough. 'I've been a real jackass about this whole affair. You were right, of course. I was doing and thinking everything that you said. But somehow—in spite of everything that I thought I knew about you, Sara, I have this compulsion to put my arms around you, to cherish you!'

'Probably something like good old-fashioned lust!' she mumbled through the silent tears.

'Perhaps,' he replied humbly. He ground out the cigarette. 'Or perhaps—Sara, I would be the first to tell you that I don't understand this conversation. Can we start again? If I ask you some direct questions, would I get a true answer?'

She thought about it, nibbling on her lip. Then she put both feet flat on the floor and stared out through the windshield. 'I'm not sure,' she answered. 'I have to admit that I lie—mostly because I hate to hurt people I do try to be honest otherwise. Ask, and we'll find out.'

'O.K. First of all, do you like me?'

'I don't know you very well,' she stammered, as her brain raced. Do I like him? Every time he comes near me I blow a fuse. Is it possible to love a man, and yet not like him? And then, because his eyes were boring a hole in her head, she said, 'Yes. I think I like you very much indeed.' Which was only half a lie.

'Does it matter that I'm so much older than you? Do you think of me as some sort of a father-figure?'

She fumbled a tiny handkerchief from her bag. Then she turned to him, reaching out to touch his cheek. 'I'm not sure what my emotions are,' she said sweetly, 'but no, I don't ever think of you as any sort of father-figure. Your age doesn't bother me. Remember, I'm older than——'

He laughed uproariously, changing from a remote autocratic figure to a boyish one. 'Yes, I know. You're older than I think. May I kiss you again, Sara?'

'Please do, John.' She managed to wipe away the last of her tears. 'I like it very much when you kiss me, John. And please don't ask me to analyse. Just do it!'

A few minutes later, her shaky voice almost a whisper, she said, 'If there are any more questions, John, I haven't the strength to answer them!'

He was chuckling as he helped her out of the car. He held her close, then pushed her slightly away so that he could see her face. 'One more thing,' he said. 'Robert. My brother is a fine fellow and I love him dearly. But he considers himself to be the original Don Juan. I've never ever brought a girl home without Robert stealing her from me. It's a sort of challenge to him, Sara. He thinks of it as a game, you know. And he's got a lot going for him—looks, career, accomplishments. I don't know a single thing that I've got that he hasn't got more of or better than.'

'Don't run yourself down, John,' she said. 'I know one thing that you've got that he hasn't. Me!'

He bent down and kissed the top of her head. As they went towards the front stairs he said something under his breath. Although she wasn't exactly sure, Sara was fairly positive that he had said, 'And the hell with you, Robert!'

They climbed the stairs in single file, John leading, Sara in the middle, and Mary waddling along in the rear. Like an ancient patriarch and his harem, Sara thought—and giggled. Or maybe more like a great Indian warrior and his squaw? For some reason her spirits were bubbling over, and when John stopped on the porch to sweep Jackie up in his arms, her cup ran over. She leaned back and gave an Indian war whoop, then circled the two of them in a shuffling war dance, using her right hand to her mouth to add a tremolo to the chant. 'Hail, Paleface,' she yelled, 'give um back papoose!' Then she stopped in front of him, her eyes on his shoes. They were motionless, pointing accusingly at her. Slowly she traced her eyes up the impeccable ridge of his dark pinstriped trousers, up the silver buttons of his shirt, to the craggy, stern, implacable, unsmiling face. 'Oh dear,' Sara sighed half to herself. 'Plainly we are not amused!' Impulsively she decided to attack. She leaned far enough back to be able to see his face clearly. She clasped her hands behind her back, tilting her head.

'I'll not scalp you this time,' she said primly, 'but if I ever get the chance I'm going to burn every one of your ten thousand pinstriped suits in a bonfire!'

All of which brought a startled expression to his face, and a high giggling laugh from Jackie. 'Oh, Sara,' the boy called out, 'you are funny! Isn't she, Daddy?'

But 'Daddy' said not a word, and as Sara ducked under his arm and raced up the stairs to her room she could only hear the laughter of the child. She held the bedroom door open only long enough for Mary to squeeze through, then she slammed it and leaned back against it, out of breath.

'Very funny, Pocahontas!' she hissed at herself. 'You get everything coming up roses, and then you have to play comic! Well, if you're that funny, how come you've got all the pie on your own face?'

An hour later Sara was sitting yoga-fashion in the middle of her bed, still berating herself for her stupidity, when the door to her room opened. Mary raised her head slightly, but did not even whine as little Jackie came in. He walked to the centre of the room, bowed briefly in the manner of a circus master-of-ceremonies, and announced, 'Daddy says to come to supper. At once!' And then, with an added giggle, 'They're fighting like mad down there. You better hurry, or you'll miss all the good parts!'

'Oh, lordy,' Sara complained, 'I haven't even cleaned up. I can't go like this!'

'He said "at once",' maintained Jackie stoutly. 'After you ran up the stairs he laughed. He laughed so hard that he sat down on the bottom stair and there was tears in his eyes. Come on, slowpoke!'

'Did he really?' Sara gasped. 'Well, that's no way for you to talk to your mother!' Her spirits were entirely restored. John had actually laughed!

'You're not my mother today,' Jackie enjoined. 'This is a weekend. I only hired you for weekdays.'

'Okay, barrister,' she replied, 'scoot out of here while I do my Cinderella act. Scoot!'

Fifteen minutes later, with her hair brushed and floating free, and wearing a flowing white skirt and a ruffled white blouse, she walked sedately down the stairs, with Mary padding behind her. She looked every bit of sixteen, and knew it. She flounced her skirts, and wished she had the courage to slide down the broad oak banister. The voices coming from the dining room were loud. There was an occasional aside in John's deep voice, but the majority of the argument was carried by Robert's pleasant tenor. Sara peered around the doorjamb, and John waved her into the room. He pulled her close beside him.

'I thought we'd decided to forgo the dividend,' Robert was saying.

'Yes, but I'm having second thoughts,' John commented. 'Don't you think we ought to bring in outside help, and get to the bottom of the problem? We haven't paid a dividend in the last five quarters. In two years we haven't shown a profit, yet the sales figures are higher than ever. How long will we be able to meet the payroll?'

'If you're not happy with my management,' Robert retorted, 'you can always sell your shares, you know. Don't forget, I own almost as many shares as you do, and Aunt Lucinda gave me her proxy three years ago. I was her choice to run the company. And now, I understand that Sara gets the income from them, but I suppose the voting rights are suspended?'

'Not hardly,' John replied dryly. 'All voting rights have already passed into Sara's hands.'

'I didn't understand that,' said Robert. He looked at Sara with renewed interest.

'Not so sure of yourself now, Robert? Sara's shares represent the swing vote for control right at this minute. What Sara decides, if she agrees with either one of us, goes. Sara?'

'I don't know what you both are talking about,' Sara complained. 'I've barely got my eyes open. What are the options?'

'Robert proposes that we skip the dividends, and go on the way we are. I propose that we have some outsider investigate, find out why we're not making a profit, and then take what action seems appropriate.'

'And all the information is in these two folders?'

'Yes, they are, Sara,' said Robert. 'Don't tell me you also read corporation reports?'

No, I certainly do not, Sara thought, but I bet I know a fellow who does! She rubbed her hand across her forehead to hide the gleam in her eyes. 'I suppose there are copies here that I could study? And then maybe we could discuss it again in a few days?'

'I really need a quick decision,' Robert blustered.

'When I've read the documents,' Sara insisted.

'All right,' he muttered gracelessly. He started for the door, giving Mary a wide berth. Then he stopped. 'I won't stay for supper, John—it's not worthwhile. But Sara, you and I ought to become better acquainted. Have you seen anything of the countryside?' She shook her head. 'Well, how about tomorrow? We could take an afternoon on my boat, go up and down the river, you know. Then a little picnic, perhaps?'

'Not tomorrow, Robert,' she replied. 'I'm too tired. Make that tomorrow week?' She looked over her shoulder for John's approval. He smiled and nodded agreement.

'You don't have to ask him for approval, damn it,' Robert snorted. 'You're a big girl now. You really are a big girl now. Whatever gave me the idea that you were just a child? Well, I've got to run. See you!'

'He's driving a Ferrari tonight,' Sara commented casually as they walked back into the house. 'A Delorian yesterday, a Ferrari today, and a boat on the river?'

'Oh, come on, Sara,' John chided her. 'Are you trying to make my little brother into some sort of monster? So he likes cars. Want a drink before supper?'

'A little orange juice, perhaps. Or some ginger ale would be nice.'

'I have all kinds of alcohol, Sara, and now that we're in agreement about how old you are, you could have a real drink.'

'No, I don't drink alcohol, John. It killed my father. And for that matter, I guess, my mother too.'

'Ah, I begin to understand better,' he said.

'No, you don't, John. You don't understand me one tiny little bit. But one of these days I'm going to make you. One of these days.'

'But right now I think we'd better go and round up Jackie and have supper. Drink up!'

After supper John pleaded work and disappeared. Jackie watched TV, a re-run of a popular police show. Sara sat down on the bottom step in the hall and tried to reason out her position. 'You're a terrible juggler, she told herself. You've told so many lies—well, half-truths, that you don't know what street you are on. Too many apples in the air. One more and the whole shebang is going to collapse, and you with it!' At which point her subconscious mind intruded and said, 'And then we can all go home and forget this crazy place!' And Sara said out loud, 'The devil we can!'

'Sara,' said Jackie as he came out of the TV room, 'why are you sitting on the stairs talking to yourself?'

'Mmm? Oh, Jackie!' She cuddled the little boy to her. 'Honest Injun? There's no one around here dumb enough to understand what I mean, so I have to talk to myself.'

'Oh, Sara,' he said disgustedly, 'you're funny!'

She got up, clutching his hand. 'Is that funny ha-ha,

or funny—peculiar?' she asked. 'Come on, let's go and get your bath.'

'But Mrs Emory is supposed to give me my bath, Sara!' he protested.

'But Mrs Emory has got her feet up, and she's watching that new night-time soap opera. You afraid I might wash you away?'

'No, silly,' he replied as they started up the stairs. At the top he paused suspiciously. 'Sara,' he said, 'you know that mothers are *supposed* to give baths? You understand I'm not paying extra for this?'

'That's all right, Champ,' she chuckled. 'This is for free. I'm practising. I'm thinking seriously of going into the mommy business full time, and I need the practice.'

Neither of them noticed that John was standing in his bedroom doorway as they rattled down the hall. In the bathroom Sara turned on the taps while Jackie struggled to get out of his shirt.

'You might try to unbutton the buttons,' Sara suggested as the little boy struggled with his head caught in an arm hole. 'Hold still, for goodness' sake, or you'll strangle yourself! Now, into the tub.' The boy smiled at her and climbed gingerly into the tub. In less than two minutes they were engaged in a water-fight, so that it was hard to tell whether the boy-child in the tub was older than the girl-child on the floor.

'But you'll never escape me,' Sara screeched, as she moved towards him with a well-soaped face cloth. 'I am Mrs Clean, the monster that devoured Chicago!'

'And you'll never get me!' he responded, diving under the water and accomplishing all that the threatening facecloth had proposed.

'Watch closely, little mortal,' she yelled as he came up for air, 'I'm about to make your world vanish!' She raised both hands over her head and wiggled them like tentacles.

'Is this a family fight, or can anyone join?' John came into the bathroom.

'Oh!' Sara exclaimed, nonplussed. 'Er—anyone can join, providing they pay their own cleaning bills—sir.'

'Come on, Daddy,' the boy shouted. 'Your turn!' And he threw a wet facecloth which, by sheer luck, hit his father on the side of his head.

'O.K., you guys,' Sara called ten minutes later, after being the recipient of two more wet cloths. 'O.K. now, the party's over What a mess you've made—we've made!'

'Sara's a grouch,' they both began chanting, 'a grouch, a grouch, a grouch!'

'Oh, sure,' she retorted disgustedly, 'but Sara the grouch has to clean up all this mess. Mrs Emory has gone to bed. Unless, of course, you really believe in the equality of the sexes and are willing to clean it up yourselves?'

Both of them stopped the soapsuds war, looked a little sheepish, but failed to volunteer for the cleaning job. Sara hid her own smile and snatched up the huge bathtowel from the rack. She wrapped the little boy in it from head to toe, and then gestured to John. He swung Jackie, towel and all, over his shoulder, and together the three of them went into the bedroom, where the boy was unceremoniously dumped on the bed. John began to rub him briskly through the towel. Then he took the wide edge of the towel and flipped Jackie out on to the bed.

'Bare behind gets a free whack,' Sara called as she patted him gently on his bottom. He squirmed off to the side of the bed, rolling with laughter. 'Not fair,' he roared. 'That's no bare behind. I'm sitting on it!' Nevertheless he rushed to shove his legs into his Superman pyjamas, then crawled back on to the bed. Sara pulled back the covers and helped him inside. He lay there, clutching his teddy bear, watching the two adults who stood side by side at his bed.

John casually put his arm around Sara's shoulder and tousled her hair. 'Ain't it swell, Daddy,' the little boy exclaimed. 'Doesn't Sara make a wonderful mommy? Are you gonna read to me now, Sara?'

She laughed at him, and ducked under John's arm. 'Nope,' she replied. 'Your daddy will read to you. This mommy has to dry up the bathroom.' She leaned over and kissed his little nose.

'How about me?' John asked.

'I can't reach!' Sara replied.

'So I'll bend over.' But Sara had already fled.

As she swabbed the bathroom, using the towels which were already partially wet, she could hear the sound of John's deep voice, punctuated by Jackie's giggles. For some reason a feeling of deep contentment filled her. By the time she had restored some semblance of order to the bathroom, John came through.

'He's asleep,' he reported. 'Why don't we go downstairs and relax together, Sara?' He pulled her close to him, and with his arm on her shoulder, and hers around his waist, they went downstairs. He stopped at the door to the sitting-room and turned her around to face him.

'You do Jackie a lot of good,' he told her. 'I haven't seen him so happy in years.'

'It's you who must do him good,' she replied softly. 'He needs a mother. He needs someone to love him, someone who'll be here every day. If you want to cure him of his troubles, find him a mother.'

'Are you applying for the job, Sara?'

'It might be nice,' she answered wistfully, 'but there's more to it than that, you know.'

John reflected for a moment. 'You like children, Sara?'

'Of course.' She moved back into the shelter of his arms. 'They've been my major interest for years.'

'Plan to have any of your own?' he teased.

'Of course,' she said absently, somewhat bemused by his closeness. 'If I ever find the right man. I always thought three would be a nice number.'

'Ah,' he said, and for some reason that one little word brought a happy glow to Sara's starved heart.

CHAPTER SIX

SARA woke up on Monday morning in sections. First a faint stirring in the legs, then a flex of the arms, next slowly force one eye open, and then turn on the ears. She could hear an argument outside the window between a pair of finches and the chickadees, and could smell the heavy sweetness of the lilacs. She savoured it all before opening the other eye. She showered, trying to avoid waking Jackie. Then she brushed her hair and teeth, put on her favourite bathrobe, and stumbled downstairs.

The kitchen was empty. She made and drank three cups of instant coffee, and chewed on a piece of toast. Then, having restored herself to life, she marched back upstairs. Jackie was awake by this time. He came into her room, bounced on her bed, and arm-wrestled her. Sara hustled him into the shower, laid out his school clothes, and then started on the task of transforming herself into a typical suburban mother. By the time Jackie had struggled into his own clothes, Sara was ready.

She had chosen a denim skirt, and a frilly cotton blouse combination in blue and white. Her hair was braided in two plaits and then fastened, coronet style, close to her head. She added her only pair of panty-hose, a pair of flat shoes, a brief touch of lipstick, and her horn-rimmed glasses. But as she paraded herself in front of her mirror, she knew that something important was missing. She rummaged through her tiny jewellery box, unstrung her mother's wedding ring from the gold chain on which she kept it, and slipped it on her left ring finger.

'You sure make a pretty mommy,' Jackie told her from the doorway. 'I hope you don't make a mess of it!'

'You've got a nerve,' she retorted. 'Don't ruin my confidence before the curtain goes up!'

'We don't have no curtains at school,' he rejoined. 'They took them all down for cleaning.'

'All right, smart alec,' she grinned. 'Let's go downstairs for your breakfast, and then we'll try out the act. Ready?'

Three-quarters of an hour later she and the boy scrambled into the VW, with Mary squeezed in the back seat. Sara looked down at Jackie enquiringly. He gave her the thumbs-up sign, and they started off.

The Frontier Regional School was at the far end of town, so their drive took them past the electronics plant. Sara was whistling a tune from *HMS Pinafore*, much to Mary's distress.

'Lookit, Sara,' Jackie called. 'Look at the plant. There's something going on there!'

Sara slowed the car to a crawl and looked over to her right. 'It looks like a picket line,' she said. 'I think there's a strike at the plant. Did your daddy or Uncle Robert mention it?'

'Nope,' he responded. 'Turn left here on Main Street, Sara. The school is just down the street.' Sara resumed speed, moving in a heavier flow of traffic, all of it apparently bound for the school complex. She was lucky to find a parking space just in front of the Tilton library, and only around the corner from the school. She backed the little car skilfully into the space and killed the engine.

'Okay, troops,' she called, 'this is it. Synchronise watches! Everybody outside for the main show. And Mary, if you scare a single kid I'll fry you for lunch. You hear me?' The big dog licked her hand, unbothered by the threat.

Jackie opened the door on his side and stepped out on to the concrete sidewalk. Mary followed. Sara squeezed out on her side, and led them around the corner to the small circular driveway that gave access to the main school doors. Here she squatted down on her heels in front of the boy.

'Are any of them looking?' she whispered. He nodded. She reached over and brushed some crumbs from his sweater. 'This is where I tell you to behave yourself and don't get in any fights, and don't get your clothes dirty,' Sara continued. 'Come on! Smile and say yes.' The boy complied. 'And this is where I tell you to study hard and do what you're told,' and she shook her finger under his nose.

He giggled back at her. 'Yes, Mommy,' he chortled.

'And this is the mushy part,' she said as she swept him off his feet and kissed him soundly. The little arms remained around her neck considerably longer than the drama required, and when he leaned back and said, 'Yes, Mommy,' there were the tiniest tears in his eyes. She put him down on the ground, and he took one hesitant step towards the door and stopped.

'You see those two big kids by the door, Sara,' he whispered. 'That's the same two. Did you want to walk to the door with me, Sara?' He was offering a solution which he obviously hated.

'No indeed,' Sara replied. 'That would be sissy stuff.'

'Yeah.' He looked around the area reflectively. 'You better wait a while, Sara,' he commented. 'I better—I may be going home early again.'

'I wouldn't think so,' she answered soberly. She picked up one of his small hands and tucked it into Mary's collar. 'Go, Mary!' she commanded. 'Guard!' She stood up, patted Jackie gently on his bottom, and brushed off her skirt.

The little boy and the big black dog marched proudly together through the crowd of waiting children. Nobody ran, nobody screamed, but it seemed that a path opened in front of them without any command, and remained open behind them for a short time. Sara heard Mary pad her part by whuffing as she came up to the two boys whom Jackie had pointed out. Both of them, almost a foot taller than Jackie, stumbled quickly backwards. One tripped over the low wire fence that protected the flower bed, and fell into a rose bush. When the boy and the dog reached the school door Jackie said something to the teacher who was serving as monitor. Then he hugged the dog, and pointed back towards Sara. As the dog ambled away the boy stood in the school door and watched.

Sara struggled with the giggles. 'Mary, you old fraud,' she whispered, 'what part are you playing now? Lassie? Get in the car, you old fake, before some cat comes along and scares you half to death!' But once they were both inside the car she whooped and gave the dog a hug. 'Very satisfactory,' she added, 'Very satisfactory!'

A quick look at her watch showed that it was too early for her to do some much-needed shopping, so she drove back towards the house, only to have her attention caught again by the picket line at the factory. Curious, she drove into the executive parking lot and got out. A couple of the pickets who had started for her car stopped when they saw the sheer size of Mary unfolding from the back seat. Sara walked over to them, her hand tight on Mary's collar. The strike was peaceful. Pickets were talking to each other, and the two policemen on duty looked bored. But no one was crossing the picket line.

Sara walked over to the nearest picket, a girl of her own age. 'I'm the new nurse,' she said. 'What's the trouble?'

The girl looked her over. 'Ellen Southern,' she said. 'She got burned at that open chemical bath we've been complaining about for the last year. Nobody's going back in until there've been some changes!' Sara waved casual acknowledgment and walked towards the separate door of the clinic, holding her Nursing I.D. card up. Pickets waved her through.

Dr Fineberg was walking down the hall as she came in. 'What are you doing here?' he exclaimed.

'I saw the confusion and thought you might need someone to give you a hand. Anything I can do?'

'You're just what I need. There's only one patient, but it's a woman. None of the rest of my staff has come in, and she is terribly embarrassed. Acid burns.' Sara followed him down the hall as he talked. 'I'm keeping her arm and shoulder bandaged with material soaked in a neutraliser. I want to change the bandage one more time, and then we'll send her down to Springfield to the burn centre.'

Sara washed thoroughly, then squirmed into the clinical jacket he offered, and spent the next ten minutes assisting as he carefully removed and replaced the heavily soaked bandages.

'We're covering it again just for the trip, Ellen,' the doctor explained. 'Down at the hospital they'll neutralise the entire area more thoroughly. Now, while I fix up your records, Nurse Anderson will get you dressed and out to the ambulance.' He gestured towards the door, behind which a siren heralded the arrival of the ambulance.

Sara helped the girl up off the examination table, draped her blouse and coat over her gently, and steadied her as she walked to the door. There was scattered applause from the picket line as the two girls walked the few paces to the ambulance. Sara stayed at Ellen's side until the ambulance attendants took over, then she went back to the clinic. Just as her hand reached for the door knob a much larger hand brushed hers aside.

'What the hell are you doing here in that get-up, Sara?' She blinked up at the sunlit dark-suited figure and shrugged her shoulders. It obviously was just not her day!

'Why aren't you off teaching school?' she countered. John pushed her roughly through the door, then whirled her around. 'Don't you know *anything*!' he shouted at her. She shrank away from him and covered both her ears. 'That picket line could explode at any minute. A girl has been hurt, and they're angry! And I suppose you walked calmly up to the line and they all waved you through?'

'You don't have to be sarcastic. That's exactly what happened,' she said, struggling to keep her voice from squeaking. 'I walked up to the picket line and told them who I was, and they all smiled and waved me through.' For some reason she was beating on his chest with her little fists. 'Every time we meet, John, you seem to put some evil or stupid interpretation on what I'm doing—and I'm sick of it. Leave me alone! Let go of me!'

'I'll let go of you,' he snarled between clenched teeth, 'just after I've shaken some sense into that beautiful head of yours!' His steel fingers shook her back and forth until she began to panic. Without thinking she raised her right foot and slammed it down on the top of his instep with all the force her tiny body could muster. He was more surprised than hurt. His arms fell away, and he hopped on one foot, muttering under his breath. Sara looked appalled, but then self-righteousness prevailed. She ran her hand through her hair, rearranged her blouse, sniffed at him, and walked through the nearest door.

It led, purely by chance, to the executive offices of the plant. Well, as long as I'm here, Sara thought, I might as well see how the other of the Bobbsy twins lives. She followed the signs to the door which was tastefully labelled 'President.' When she opened the door she found herself in a secretarial office. The only occupant was reading a newspaper.

'Mr Englewood?' she enquired. 'Please tell him that Sara Anderson is here.'

'Go right in,' the secretary said. 'He's never busy.'

'I guess the strike has slowed things down?' Sara asked.

'No, it's always like this,' the secretary replied. 'Is that wolf with you?'

'Not really,' Sara replied sweetly. 'It's more correct to say that I'm with her.' She snapped her fingers at Mary and walked over to the inner door. She debated knocking, then decided not to. She pushed her way into the inner office.

For a business office in a small plant it was a huge affair. Great carpeted spaces were occasionally interrupted by scattered upholstered chairs. One desk, of huge proportions, sat before the bay windows at the far end. In the middle of the room, practising his golf putting, was Robert Englewood. He looked up when the door closed behind Sara and Mary. An astonished expression ran across his face, then he recovered and his best smile snapped into place. He dropped his club and came to her with outstretched arms.

'Sara, me darling,' he said in his hypnotic voice. 'What a wonderful thing to come and see me!' Mary growled. He stopped. 'I thought you might have got rid of that beast,' he said, not so happily. 'But—well, it's good to see you, Sara. Come over here and sit down. A drink?'

She shook her head, but followed him to an overstuffed sofa. He sat close to her, resting one arm on the back of the sofa. Mary walked around behind them and rested her head between them.

'I saw the excitement outside when I drove past,' Sara said. 'I thought I would see how things were going.'

'Excitement?' he asked blandly.

'The strike—you know. The pickets and the police and all that.'

'Oh, that,' he dismissed it all with a wave of his hand. 'A minor problem. The union has been itching for a fight for a couple of weeks. One of my staff is attending to it.'

'But why are they on strike, Robert?' she persisted.

'The usual things, Sara. Money, hours, holidays, cost of living bonuses—the usual stuff. We've been negotiating for the past three weeks. I have a team that does that for me.'

'I understand that one of your employees has been injured,' she said. 'I suppose you want to know all about that at once?'

'Oh, I do, Sara,' he assured her. 'I certainly do. But I have three-hundred and fifty-two employees here, you know, so I'm always busy. Look at that stack of papers on my desk.' He moved closer to Sara, but Mary lowered her head further between them, and he drew back. Sara got up from the sofa and walked over to the desk. On top of the pile of papers was an opened copy of the *Daily Racing News*.

'Organisation, Sara,' he said, coming around to stand beside her.

She moved a few steps away from him. 'I've really got to go, Robert. I only have a moment.' She tried out one of her sunniest smiles on him, and walked towards the door.

'Don't forget our date for next Sunday,' he called after her. 'Picnic lunch, a day on the water, and then we'll go up to my little pad for a swim in the pool.'

The outer office was as quiet as before. The secretary looked up briefly from her newspaper and watched as Sara and Mary went out into the corridor. In the distance Sara could see a figure that looked very much like John, coming towards her. 'This is no time for conversations,' she told herself. 'I must learn never to get near him when he's angry! But then he only seems to get angry when I get close to him!' She tugged off the clinical coat, dropped it in the nearby waste container, and fled in the other direction, towards the main entrance.

Sara clutched Mary's collar tightly as she made her way back to the parking lot. None of the pickets turned in her direction. She pushed the dog into the back seat and drove out on to the highway. After a few yards, unable to make up her mind, she pulled off the road on to the dry shoulder, and shut off the engine. She had two options, she thought. She could go downtown, cash a couple of her travellers cheques, and buy some clothes to replace the late lamented shifts. Or she could turn the other way, drive home, corner Mrs Emory in the kitchen, and really learn something about this whole crew of kooks with whom she was now associated!

Or she could sit still, right here, and daydream. Dear

John! Strange how she could be thinking about him in those terms. On Thursday he had been a stranger who had kissed her on the beach. On Friday he was that angry man who had flown her to this far place—and shared a bed with her. On Saturday he was a madman, disgusted with her, and she loved him just the same. On Sunday he had gone to church, while she avoided him in order to make a critical telephone call. And here it was Monday, and he was 'Dear John'. But what a homely, opinionated, beastly, hateful, strong, loving—it made no sense! Sara shook herself back to attention, turned on the motor, and drove back to the farmhouse.

Mrs Emory was in the kitchen when Sara breezed in. She had completed all her basic work towards dinner and supper, and was now absorbed in coffee and doughnuts.

'There's a man waiting for you in the library,' Emma said. 'He said your brother telephoned him on Sunday. Why don't you bring him in here?'

'Oh, I will, Emma,' Sara squealed. 'It's Packy, I'll bet. Packy Muldoon!' She rushed out of the kitchen and returned a moment later arm in arm with a short round elderly man. His smile was as big as a house, his hair as sparse as a desert, and a gold tooth gleamed on the right side of his mouth.

'Emma,' Sara said excitedly, 'let me introduce you to Dr Padraic Muldoon.'

'People call me Packy, Emma,' he said.

'And what kind of a doctor are you?' Emma asked.

'Companies,' he laughed. 'I doctor sick companies. And Sara, pigeon—your brother was terribly angry with you when he called me last night.' He sat down at the table and picked up a doughnut. 'You'll not believe, Mrs Emory, what a scheming sharp-tongued little girl this one is.'

'Ralph is my brother in Boston, Emma,' Sara explained. 'He's the father of Pudge. You remember I told you? And why is my oldest brother so mad, Packie?'

'Because, me love, it is not the thing to say of the Chairman of the Massachusetts State Lottery Commision that he's in the numbers racket! Ah, do you have the grace to blush, hey?'

'Well, he came over all big-brotherish, and I know if I let him get away with it I'd never have a moment's peace. And he *is* in the numbers racket, isn't he?'

'Ah well, now. I have known Ralph, man and boy, for thirty years and more, and he does get a little stuffy. But I have to be in Springfield by one o'clock this afternoon, Sara. What's the problem?'

'Packy, there's this company up here. I own a piece of it, and it doesn't seem to make a profit. Wait just a minute. Emma could you buy Packy a cup of coffee and a doughnut?'

Sara whisked out of the room, and was back almost immediately, with two printed pamphlets in her hand. The two older people had already struck up a friendship.

'Lovely doughnuts,' Packy complimented, as he chomped on a sugar-coat, with honey and nuts. 'You make this all yourself?'

'Away with you!' the housekeeper laughed. 'Fresh and homemade—from the Mister Donut shop in town. Frank picks up a package every day on his way back from delivering the eggs. Nobody bakes like this at home any more. Although occasionally I do have a hand at a batch of fresh bread.'

'Here's the problem, Packy,' Sara interrupted. 'This first report is from three years ago. The company made a handsome profit that year. Here's this year's report.'

'Ah, will you look now,' Packy Muldoon chuckled. 'Pretty pictures and lots of pages. I suppose there's a very limited distribution of these reports? My, what a very large haystack!'

'I think John said there are only ten copies. Most of the stock is owned by three people. Why a haystack?'

'For hiding pins in, my dear,' he laughed. 'A very common approach. Why don't you all have a gossip, while I take this material over here in the corner and have a look-see.'

There was silence for a moment, and then, trying to cover the conversational gap, Mrs Emory said, 'You're not exactly a stranger in a kitchen, are you, Sara?'

'Not exactly,' Sara mumbled through a mouthful of doughnut. 'There were four of us children, you know, and I was the only girl. Papa kept the boys hopping day and night. And Mamma said a girl's place was not necessarily in the kitchen, but at least she had to know how to make do. And I'll tell you, she put me through the high hoops. I can cook and bake and sew and clean. But not as good as Mamma. Dear Mamma, I miss her so.'

Mrs Emory pulled her chair closer and patted Sara's hand. 'There now, girl,' she said. 'Has she been long gone?'

'Not long. Just over two months ago. And now it's just me and the boys—and Pudge, of course, and Sylvia, and Jim's wife Alice, and—I guess I must have cried an ocean.'

'Tell me about it, Sara. It always helps.' The older woman refilled both their coffee cups and sat back.

'Well,' Sara mused, 'it all began with Papa. He was a doctor too, a general practitioner. He worked hard, didn't get rich, but loved us all. And Mamma, of course, was much more famous than Papa. She was one of the top surgeons in New England, at the top of her profession. Isn't that funny? My mamma would spend four hours on a complicated lung surgery, and then come home and teach me how to bake French bread. She used to say that a man could be a doctor or a lawyer or an Indian chief, but a woman had to be a woman first. Strange.'

Sara stopped and sipped her coffee, her mind two hundred miles away. The only sound in the kitchen was the ticking of the wall-clock, and the clack of the keys of the little pocket calculator that Packy Muldoon was using.

'And so one day Papa went out to mail a letter, and a drunk in a ten-year-old car smashed into him. It crushed his chest. They rushed him to the hospital, the same hospital where Mamma was on duty as chief surgeon. She didn't even know who the patient was. She looked at the X-rays, scrubbed up, and went into the operating room. And she just couldn't do it. She just couldn't lay a knife on the man she loved—not even to save his life. So they called in someone else, but Papa died before they could finish the operation. That same day Mamma took down her shingle, and never ever treated another patient again. She just seemed to disappear inside herself, and finally, a year after Papa died, she just didn't wake up one morning. In a way, I'm glad she's gone. For her—life without him was too painful to bear!'

'Ah, but there's tragedy in every family,' Emma commented.

'Wasn't there something here? With John's wife?' Sara probed.

'Oh, that one!' Mrs Emory exclaimed. 'That one was a real cross that the poor Professor had to bear. Believe me, if she'd been my child I would have drowned her when she was a kitten!'

'Then why did he come to marry her?'

'Who knows why a man marries? He met her at university—he was only an instructor then. She was in one of his classes, too old to be a student, strictly a manhunter. Oh, a pretty one, mind you, all tall and blonde and blue eyes, thin as a whippet, knew how to dress. But she never stopped chasing men—even after the wedding. When the Professor brought her out here to live, when they were expecting the boy, she thought it was the end of the world. Until she met Robert and his friends, and then she took to the bottle. Fell down the stairs, she did. I'll bet a nickel she was as drunk as a skunk. Nobody here in the house but her and the boy, you know. The Professor was down at the University. Somebody called the police—and that was a queer thing. They never did find out who made that call. But there she was, at the bottom of the stairs, with her neck broken. And the poor little boy shaking her, trying to get her to wake up. Only six he was then. The child never recovered, until you came, that is. You're good for him.'

'That must have been terrible,' Sara said softly. 'I suppose Robert came over and took charge?'

'Him? Him that can't stand the sight of blood? Luckily he was gone on a trip to Florida—or so his secretary said. Funny thing, too. When I went upstairs, after the ambulance and all, all her clothes were packed. A couple of suitcases were sitting by her door.'

'And then what happened?'

'The Professor was that upset! Shut himself up in the library for four days after the funeral, then came out and ordered me to pack everything of hers. Every stitch and bauble, mind you. He gave it all to the Salvation Army—a clean sweep, nothing left in the house of her or hers. And not a word spoken, morning to night, about the whole affair. It's worth your head, Sara, to mention the subject under this roof. Except with me, of course.'

The two of them sat shaking their heads at each other. Sara picked up her coffee cup. It had grown cold. She topped it off from the pot.

'Fill mine too,' Packy Muldoon said. 'A weasel of a report here, Sara.'

'You've solved the problem so soon?' Sara exclaimed.

'No,' he laughed, 'I don't have a solution. But I can tell you what the problem is. Will that do, Acushla?'

'Yes, Packy, that will do. Ralph always said you were a wizard.'

'This is a pretty amateur attempt,' he said, tapping the two reports with his fingers. 'The people who made up this report were playing the old shell game. But of course there's only so many shells you can hide the pea under, aren't there? Here's your problem, Sara. Your plant is making a very tiny but valuable item.

Customers are lined up ten deep for this stuff, including a lot of countries behind the Iron Curtain. So look here. This year you produced four times as many units as you did three years ago. Your costs—raw materials, labour, overheads—all that stuff, have gone up ten per cent. But your sales records don't match the amount of goods the plant produced. So that means, Sara, one of several things. First, that you have so much spoilage in your manufacturing that you have a mile-high junk heap behind your plant. Or second, that your salesmen are selling at cut-rate prices, or third, that your warehouse is crammed to the roof with the stuff. Or fourth, Sara, that twenty-five per cent of your inventory is sliding out the back door of the plant!'

'But I—but that can't be, Packy.' How could anyone steal that much material?'

'Remember the size of these things, Sara. Five thousand of them could fit into the back of a station wagon. All you need is a leaky security system, a fast truck, and a fence willing to handle this kind of thing. Tremendous profits, Sara—tremendous. But I've got to go. Where's my hat?'

'You never wear a hat, Packy Muldoon, and you know it!'

'Yes, well—and Sara, next time you call that brother of yours in the numbers racket, give him my regards, hey?'

Sara walked him to the door, then returned to the kitchen. She and Mrs Emory spent the remainder of the morning and the early afternoon working side by side, and talking companionably. When the wall clock struck two-thirty, it startled Sara.

'Excuse me, Emma,' she called as she threw her apron in the general direction of a wall hook. 'I forgot all about the school. It's out at three, and I promised Jackie I wouldn't be late. Not on my first day on the job!'

Mary was so soundly asleep under the kitchen table

that it took several nudges to awaken her. The two of them dashed for the Bug and were on their way. The pickets were still at the plant, Sara noted, but she had no time to spare. Barely on the moment she jammed the VW into a parking space in front of Congregational Church. Some of the older children were already out of school. Small groups of parents were gathered, waiting for the younger classes to be released.

Sara missed seeing Jackie come through the door. The younger classes were brought out in groups, in column of twos rather than being released as individuals. It was Mary who first recognised the boy. He was marching at attention, with eyes straight ahead, as were all the other small children.

'Go, Mary,' Sara commanded. The big dog sniffed, and loped over to the column. She worked her way down the line until she came to Jackie, then turned and matched step for step with the column until it reached the sidewalk. At the dismissal command boy and dog broke out like rockets and flashed to where Sara waited for them. She managed to catch Jackie as he jumped the last two feet at her. She swung him up over her head, then hugged him. With his mouth at her ear he whispered, 'Sara? You're the prettiest mom in the whole class, and Mrs Sedgewick wants to meet you, and will you come to class and bring Mary and tell all the kids about guard dogs and you didn't kiss me!'

'Whoa!' Sara laughed. 'First the kissing bit!' and she smacked him gently on each cheek. 'And now for the other part. Where do we find Mrs Sedgewick?'

'You're supposed to put me down,' he whispered fiercely. 'You have to keep the mush stuff down!' She gently dropped him to his feet. He reached for her hand, and slipped his other arm over Mary's neck. 'Over here,' he urged.

Mrs Sedgewick turned out to be a woman of middle age, somewhat stocky, with hair fast greying, and an attractive smile on her face. When Jackie introduced them, Sara held out her only free hand, her left, and squeezed the proffered hand of the teacher.

'It certainly is wonderful for Jackie to have a mother,' Mrs Sedgewick gushed, looking down at Sara's hand. 'You can't believe what a change it's made in the classroom today!'

'You mean my child is a troublemaker?' Sara laughed, taking the sting out of the words.

'Aw, Mom!' Jackie interjected.

'No, not a troublemaker, but you know, Jackie, many days you come to school but you're not really here. And today you won the gold star in arithmetic. All year long you've been telling me it's impossible for you to do arithmetic!'

'Jackie and I will have a little talk about that when we get home,' Sara promised. 'Now, what's this about my dog?'

'Yes, your dog. We try to enliven our classes at every chance, you know. And the performance of your— guard dog?'

'Yes. She's not a pet, she's a trained guard dog.'

'That's been the topic of all the conversations in the school today—in the cafeteria, in the teachers' lounge, and even in the Principal's meeting. The whole school is talking about Jackie and his guard dog. Could you possibly come and demonstrate, and speak to the children?'

'I would really like to,' Sara replied. 'Mary is a very old dog, but she still loves to perform. Of course you understand that this is only a tentative acceptance. I couldn't do anything without the approval of Mr Englewood.'

'If you would let me know as soon as possible?' the teacher asked. 'I'm sorry to rush you, but I really can't stay another minute—I get a lift with two other teachers. May I introduce them?' Sara agreed, and was made known to two more of the staff, both younger than Mrs Sedgewick by many years. 'And now, Jackie,' the teacher said, 'I have to agree with you. You've come up with the prettiest mother in the school. And at the next School Committee meeting I must be sure to tell your father so!'

She turned away with her two companions, leaving Sara in a state of shock. As they left, she could hear one of them say to the others, 'Can you imagine that? She can't do anything without asking her husband's permission. I thought that went out with the bloomers and the midi-blouse!'

Sara stood absolutely still, her face a brilliant sunset red. 'Are you coming, Sara?' Jackie asked. 'Everybody else has gone. I wanna go home and have a snack.'

Sara shook her head and tried desperately to still the clamour of panic going off inside her skull. 'Jackie,' she moaned, 'I think we've just put both our feet in my mouth. If your father hears about this it will be Katy-bar-the-door. He'll be using me to wipe up the floor of the barn! Come on, you two, get in the car!'

She pushed them both hurriedly into the little car, landing Mary on her head between the seats. After a few complaints and considerable sorting out, they each found a place to sit down.

'I don't see no trouble, Sara,' the boy smiled up at her. 'It went real good today. And that Bill Fenwick— that big guy—he tried to stop me in the hall again today, and I told him if he didn't watch out I'd have Mary eat him. You should have seen his face!'

'That's not the problem I was talking about,' she mused, her brain scanning desperately for solutions. 'Did you hear what Mrs Sedgewick said? At the next School Committee meeting. She thinks I'm married to your daddy. If he ever finds out about this he'll skin me six ways from Sunday!'

'What's the problem?' Jackie insisted with little-boy logic 'All you gotta do is marry Daddy. That would be nice!'

'Oh yeah?' snorted Sara. 'Men usually like to ask, not to be told! Yesterday I was sure he wouldn't touch me with a ten-foot pole. *Now* I think that's just what he'll use to beat me with!'

'But you know one good thing, Sara?' the little boy continued. She looked down at him inquisitively. 'If you marry Daddy, I could save a nickel a week!'

CHAPTER SEVEN

THAT first Monday had set the pattern for the week to come. Each morning Sara took Jackie in to school. Each day she passed the picket line at the plant and noticed that faces were growing more grim. She spent the middle of each day with Mrs Emory, helping in the house where she could, taking long walks across the farm when the weather permitted. Each evening followed a precious routine. John would be back from the University by five o'clock. They would eat supper together. splash through the hilarity of a bath routine with Jackie, and then, when the old house had settled into darkness, she would spend the late evening sitting with John in front of the fireplace, making commonplace talk while he graded papers and she worked on her sewing.

Twice she tried to steer the conversation around to the plant and the strike. 'I don't know anything about it, Sara. I hardly ever go over there. That's Robert's work—he's trained to do it. Forget it, why don't you?'

'I can't forget it, John. It's there every time I drive Jackie to school and back. There's going to be big trouble, I can see it coming. And besides, I'm a stockholder too, aren't I?'

'Yes, you are, Sara,' he commented absentmindedly, his eyes on the paper in his lap. 'Do what you please, but don't bother me.'

'Well!' she muttered under her breath. 'Be a good little girl, Sara. Run and play with your dolls. I *will* do something about it. And you'll be sorry, John Englewood!'

'Hmm?' he enquired.

'Oh, nothing,' she responded. 'I lost my place in the pattern.' Then she got up and went out, carefully closing the door behind her. And she made another long-distance telephone call.

On Thursday night they varied the pattern. John took her to a meeting of the Board of Selectmen. She was not really surprised to discover that John was First Selectman. And the calm careful manner he used in handling each subject on the warrant, as well as the respect the other town leaders evinced towards him, gave her a shiver of delight.

On Friday night he was waiting in the sitting room without any papers in hand. 'End of the term,' he explained. 'Nothing left now but Departmental examinations, and I have a group of graduate students to supervise those.'

'Must be nice,' Sara commented. She had put her gros-point away, and was working on an embroidery project around the hem of a new skirt which she had bought. 'Rank has its privileges?'

'That too,' he retorted. He reached over and fingered her pigtails. 'Your hair looks beautiful in the firelight!' Before she could protest he had slipped the elastics off the ends of her braids and was unravelling them, combing out her long hair with his fingers.

She laughed nervously. 'Does that mean I should carry a fireplace around with me all the time?'

'I didn't mean that, you minx—you know I didn't. Your hair is so soft and smells so sweet, Sara.' He lifted a heavy swatch of her hair to his lips. 'What's that scent you have in your hair?'

'Soap and water. And Johnson's Baby Shampoo, two dollars and seventy five cents a bottle.' She had completely lost track of her pattern. The red rose she was trying to construct looked more like a miscoloured watermelon!

'Relax, Sara.' His hand began to massage the nape of her neck, and much to her surprise she did relax, slumping back against his chair, swept by a sea-tide of contentment. They sat in silence for a while. Sara laid down her needle and rested her hands in her lap.

'You've done wonders for Jackie,' John told her. 'I hardly recognise him as the same little boy. Mrs Sedgewick called me, too.'

Sara snapped away from him with a jolt. All week long she had been trying to avoid the issue of what would happen if John found out!

'What did she say?' she mumbled, not really wanting to hear.

'She said that Jackie had finally settled down, and was achieving his potential, and that 'darling Sara' was a prize of the first water and was going to tell the school all about her guard dog. And she congratulated me.'

'Oh?' This in a very cautious tone. ''What for?'

'Well, she never did say, but I suppose because my son is no longer classified with Attila the Hun. Or maybe because I so cleverly trapped Sara Anderson. Or whatever. It certainly has done Jackie a power of good to have a sister, Sara.'

'Er—John?' She hesitated at the first gate, then decided to ride madly through the course. 'I don't think he thinks of me as a sister,' she stammered.

'Oh? As what, then?'

She twisted around to look up at his craggy face. 'To tell the truth, John——'

'Ah, that would be nice! And somewhat unusual.'

'You knew?'

'After I received my third congratulation, on Wednesday morning I believe that was, I began to have a little suspicion. And then there's tonight.'

'Tonight?' she queried.

'You are a very poor conspirator, Sara. You keep forgetting the little details. Look how brightly your left hand sparkles in the firelight.'

Sara felt no need to look. She didn't dare to look. Her right hand stole quickly over to cover her left, where her mother's wedding ring still reposed.

'I couldn't help notice it when we were giving Jackie his bath tonight,' John continued. 'Your own ring?'

'My mother's ring. Why aren't you yelling at me,

John? I thought surely by the time you found out you'd want to beat me! Are you so mad that you haven't thought what to do yet?'

'I know what to do,' he chuckled. He plucked her up off her cushion, deposited her in his lap, and gently but thoroughly kissed her. She squirmed against him, running her hands up to his shoulders.

'And you're not mad at me?'

'I'm not angry with you.' He riffled his fingers through her hair again. 'For the moment it seems like a good idea!'

'For Jackie's sake?'

'Ah—yes, of course. For Jackie's sake.'

On Saturday John invited her to join him on a tour. 'I want to check on something that Frank has been telling me about the farm,' he said. 'And besides, you could see a little bit more of the area than that path you've worn back and forth to school!'

He brought the jeep around to the door and loaded Mary and Jackie in the back, saving the front seat for Sara. It was a warm May day, only a week away from the end of the month. She had dressed casually in denim skirt and cotton blouse. She had left her hair loose, fastened lightly into a ponytail, but as it brushed against her face she could not for the life of her explain why she had done that.

They drove south on the River Road, passing the electronic plant, and then going into Main Street, and the village centre.

'This once was the entire village,' John explained. 'A single wide place in the road. Old houses, with towering trees on the east side. Churches and schools and the Library on the other. That's the Congregational Church over there, or as we call it now, the United Christian Church.'

'And the one next to the library?'

'That's the English language Roman Catholic Church. We have a very large Polish population in town, and they have their own church around the corner. They came over as immigrant farm labour at the turn of the century, and now they own half the valley.'

'What's that peculiar grass plot in the middle of the street, John?'

'That's a piece of history interfering with the roadbuilders, Sara.' he pulled the car over beside the twenty by ten foot plot. 'It's a cemetery, dedicated to the memory of Captain Thomas Lathrobe and his men. He was leading eighty-four men north to join the militia at Greenfield when he was ambushed here by seven hundred Indians. 1675, that was. They buried whatever they could find of the men in one single grave.'

'But that's—the Pilgrims came to Massachusetts in 1621. You mean the white man was this far inland by 1675?'

'Better than that, Sara. The first settlements in the Valley date back to 1650. It was a very uneasy place. In fact, it was the western frontier. Beyond the Berkshires there, in upper New York, were the Indians of the Six Nations. The woodlands around here are full of little plaques memorialising some settler who lost his hair. That's why Jackie's school is called Frontier Regional. Well, we'd better push on.'

It took them ten more minutes to reach the first of the tobacco fields. Labourers were setting seedlings in the ground, under huge muslin nets that covered the entire area. 'We grow cigar tobacco,' John explained. 'If we keep it in the shade the leaf will be thinner and more delicate because of the higher moisture content. This is all a farm co-operative. I have about twenty-five acres under shade. With all our neighbours there's about four hundred acres here in the valley. The co-operative standardises the seeds and brings the seedlings up in those greenhouses you see over there. Then we all plant, and the resultant leaf is sold back to the co-op. If we're lucky, we make a bundle. If not—well, that's the story of all farming these days.'

He stopped to take up a technical discussion with his farm manager and several other consultants. They examined reports, ran the soil through their fingers, and watched the planting going forward. Several opinions were voiced, but Sara noticed that finally they all stood quietly, and waited for John. 'Very well then,' he finally told them, 'schedule another half-ton of fertiliser per acre. And spray that low-lining section again before they set the plants.' John came back to the jeep wiping his hands on his jeans, and with a start Sara realised that this was the first time she had seen him out of his dark suits!

Another fifteen-minute drive took them up a hillside into the apple orchards. The trees were beginning to bud, leaving the area with a sweet soft tang. 'Well, I didn't understand that tobacco business worth a darn,' Sara confided. 'At least all you have to do here is to pick the apples?'

'Sara, you'll never make a farmer, will you? We have to cherish these trees as if they were infants. We selected this place to plant them after a long study. They have to be out of the really cold weather, yet be cold enough so that the trees are dormant for one hundred days. There are seven different types of bugs that we need to spray against. These apples are the Delicious apples. They're worth a fortune if they come to market with firm flesh, a total red colour, and this particular shape. Miss that description by one particle and all they're good for is juice. And this year—well, look here. See these tiny larvae? The gypsy moth. They're sweeping over Massachusetts like an invading army. They don't usually take to fruit trees but they've eaten out practically everything else. And you've found the larvae on all the three hundred sample trees, Frank?'

'Every tree, John. Total.'

'Okay, Frank, see if you can hire a couple or three extra crews, and spray them all by hand.'

'Be easier, quicker, and cheaper to rent a helicopter and spray from the air, John.'

'You know we can't do that, Frank. There's only one spray that will kill the gypsy moth, and it causes cancer in humans. Spray by hand. Outfit the crews with protective clothing. Post signs at all entrances to the orchards.'

'And write off the entire crop?'

'And write off the entire crop.'

The farmer manager walked away, shaking his head. Dusk was gathering along the length and breadth of the valley. Jackie and Mary had long since disappeared, chasing each other out among the lines of sentinel trees.

'So I give up,' Sara sighed. 'All I really know is when the herring are running. I guess I'd better stick to the coast.'

'Don't say that, Sara,' pleaded John. He put one arm around her shoulders and squeezed her gently. 'I know this has been a boring afternoon for you——'

'Not boring, John—not that.'

'Well, at least it hasn't been overloaded with excitement. But look down there at the valley, Sara. Can't you see the quiet peace of the whole place?'

They stood close together, watching the sun dip behind the tips of the distant Berkshires. Sara felt an excitement in her bones, a feeling that she stood on the brink of some great discovery, if she could find the right words.

'I wanted you to see all this today,' John said solemnly, 'and then I wanted to ask you a question.'

'Yes, John?'

'Sara, I know you've spent most of your life by the ocean. I know that being over a hundred miles inland must bother you. But this beautiful place, Sara—do you think that you could be content to live here?'

She knew he was asking her much more than the words themselves. She brushed her hair back from her face, just as an excuse to give herself time to think. Within the turmoil of her own mind she sought for and finally found the answer to the unasked question.

'I—John? It would depend more on person than on

place. A woman is always—must always give up much for love.'

'Think of things the way they are, Sara. You, me, Jackie, Mary, and this lovely valley. Could you be content?'

She stirred uneasily under the weight of his arm. The soft breeze stopped, and the whole world seemed to be waiting for her answer. She sighed and leaned against him, his arms wrapped around her waist.

'Yes, John,' she almost whispered, 'I could be content.'

The tableau held until Mary and Jack, worn out by their long romp through the trees, came trailing noisily back, gasping for breath, and wanting their supper.

On Sunday, after church, they all returned home to find that Robert was waiting.

'You haven't forgotten our little date?' he asked, using a tone that seemed to say it would be inconceivable that a mere female could be *that* forgetful.

Sara asked him to wait while she changed, and went up to her room. it was a lovely warm day outside. She rummaged around in her suitcase and finally found herself a pair of hip-hugger jeans and an inscribed white T-shirt. A quick look in her mirror gave her cause to think, but she was determined to make an impression on Robert, and it was very plain the type of woman he preferred. But because it was only Robert, not John, she braided her hair into one large soft plait and draped it over her left shoulder. Another moment of search brought to light a saucy wide-brimmed straw hat, and her dark glasses. She took one more good look in the mirror, and could not control the giggles. She was still giggling when she stepped out into the hall and bumped into John.

'Are you all set for your——' he stopped in mid-sentence and glared at her. 'Sara!' he commanded gruffly. 'March yourself back into your room and put some clothes on!'

Spurred by her own guilty conscience, she snarled back at him, 'I am dressed!'

'Well, at least have the decency to go back and put on a bra,' he thundered. 'It's Sunday, you know. I won't have you running around in some sort of harlot suit on Sunday!'

'*You* won't have?' Her voice was dangerously quiet. '*You* won't have? Who the devil do you think you are? Please get out of my way. Robert is waiting.'

'Don't be a fool, woman,' he snarled. 'My brother is the biggest wolf in the Valley, and you want to go out with him dressed like the tastiest bait of the season. I won't have it!'

She pulled herself away from his restraining arm. 'You won't have it? Indeed! You have no power or authority over me, Mr Englewood. I dress as I please!' But you know darned well, she told herself, that you had some second thoughts about the T-shirt, didn't you, Sara? And even saying that you'll wear a windbreaker over it all hardly covers the subject—or you, for that matter! But the sheer impertinence of it! *He* wouldn't have it!

He grabbed her arm again. 'By God, Sara,' he shouted at her, 'I wish I had some authority over you! Let me tell you, if I were your husband I'd warm your backside for you, believe me!'

She pulled her arm free again, and assumed the chilliest mask she could muster. 'What an odd thing to say, Mr Englewood,' she retorted. 'If you were my husband you wouldn't need to beat me, you would only have to command me. But luckily for both of us, you're not, are you?' And with that she skipped by him and ran down the stairs.

When she had come into the house she had commanded Mary to stand by the front door and wait. When she returned, her dog was at the door, but had managed to corner Robert in the tiny niche behind the door itself. He was saying 'Nice doggy' in a very unbelieving tone of voice when Sara appeared.

'For goodness' sake, Sara,' he called, 'get your damn dog——' and then his eyes took in her change of clothes, and the magnificent swell of her breasts under the T-shirt. 'Sara?' he queried hesitantly. He stopped and licked his lips. 'Sara,' he tried again, 'if that's really you, would you ask your dog to stop sampling me?'

Sara snapped her fingers at Mary, who promptly lay down at her feet. She smiled at Robert. She was *determined* to have a good time. She only wished John might come with them so that he could see what a wonderful time she was determined to have! If only she could snap her fingers and have John fall in at her heel, she told herself, and that thought broke her up. She giggled uncontrollably as she slipped into her wind-breaker, took Robert's arm, and walked out to his car. He laughed too, convinced that the little sexpot at his side had finally seen the light.

He had brought the Ferrari with him this time. Sara gaped in awe, then carefully sat on the real fur of the seat-cover. 'You've got more instruments than John's aeroplane,' she told him. He smiled a superior smile. She wiggled herself into a comfortable position, prepared to be amazed.

'Impressed, Sara?' he asked as he swung his door shut.

'Very much so,' she chortled. 'John told me that you were the Big Bad Wolf, but if this is the way the Wolf lives, well——'

'Pure jealousy on his part,' Robert grinned. 'My big brother has the money for a car like this, but he doesn't have the guts to be seen in public in one. Do you have to take that mutt of yours with us?'

'Love me, love my dog,' she chided him, expecting some argument. She got none. Robert unlatched the rear seat and watched Mary struggle in. The car engine started with barely a murmur. He guided it down the drive and out on to the road with as much skill as his brother, but considerably more speed. Sara settled back into the far corner of her seat, expecting some sort of wrestling match with the wolf, but after five minutes nothing had happened, so she sat up and enjoyed the scenery.

'We're going south on Route Three,' he explained. 'We head towards Springfield, the second largest city in Massachusetts. I have my pad down there, and the boat. Warm enough?' he added.

'Everything's fine,' she said, and regretted that her hair was not blowing in the breeze. And why not? With one eye on Robert she unpinned and unbraided her hair, letting it fly out behind her in the breeze.

'That's some improvement, Sara,' he commented. They turned off the highway and followed a narrow road down towards the river. 'There's my pad.' He swung the heavy car off the road and up a circular drive. His 'pad' was a two-storey house, all glass and brick in the most modern Herschl architectural style. They stopped at the ornate entrance.

'Great globs of glittering goose-grease!' Sara stuttered. 'That's your bachelor pad?'

'That's it, Sara. Impressed? Want to look through it first?'

'I'll say!' She brought her sunniest smile to bear on him. Robert led her up the four stairs to the door, and put his open palm on a copper plate set in the door. Immediately it swung open. 'Best key in the world,' he told her. 'Only responds to my fingerprints.'

'And nobody else can open it? Suppose you *wanted* somebody else to open it? Would be embarrassing, wouldn't it?'

'You don't understand modern science, Sara. I can set it to respond to up to eight sets of prints, but at this moment it's only set for one.'

'You must think me a dunce, Robert. I don't know a thing about electronics.'

'Me neither,' he laughed, leading her into the foyer. 'But I know how to hire people who know about electronics. John's the only expert on our family. Take a look at my sunken living room.'

Sara looked, and regretted. Nothing turned her off more quickly than modern plastic furniture. She concealed her distaste, and followed him around as he enumerated the rooms on the ground floor. They stopped at the slenderly graceful wrought iron stairs that led up to the floor above. 'Come on upstairs,' he urged. 'Six bedrooms, three baths. You have to see the master bedroom!'

Don't press your luck, Sara, she told herself. He's really a nice man. He's John's brother. All men are created wolves, given a chance. Step into my parlour, said the spider. She declined his invitation.

'Another time, perhaps, Robert,' she pleaded. 'I came for a boat trip, and a boat trip I must have.'

'Indeed you must,' he laughed. He led her through the house and out the back door. A carefully maintained lawn sloped down from the brick patio behind the house, to the water's edge. A concerete pier jutted a few feet out into the river.

'That's a boat?' she asked, when she saw the craft tied up at the dock.

'Hey, this isn't the Atlantic ocean!' he replied. The boat was a twenty-five-foot flat-bottomed houseboat, with two heavy outboard motors mounted at the stern.

'Quaint little thing,' Sara commented as she stepped over the rail. 'Looks like a cheesebox on a raft—oh dear, I forgot!' she exclaimed.

'You forgot what, Sara?'

'Mary. I forgot that she really hates boats. She'll come if I order her to, but I'd rather not. Do you suppose we could leave her here at the dock, Robert? She won't wander too far, and there's plenty of drinking water available.'

'Well, I'd certainly counted on her company,' he laughed. 'Come off it, Sara. You know I'd love to have her stay behind. Give her the word, will you, before she tries to eat the boat!'

Ten minutes later they were backing out of the slip. Sara stood beside Robert at the blunted bow, where the wheel was located. 'This is the widest part of the river in Massachusetts.' He waved vaguely to the port side. 'Half a mile wide here, about twenty feet deep in the channel this year. But I've seen drought years when you would walk across most of the riverbed with dry feet. The river rises in Vermont, runs through Massachusetts, and empties into the Atlantic in Connecticut. We'll go north, against the current. Want to take the wheel?'

Sara agreed. 'It handles as if you were dragging half of Deerfield behind us,' she complained. 'Is this full speed?'

'It's the only speed, witch,' he chuckled. 'Now, watch how the speed of the river seems to pick up as we squeeze through the gorge up ahead.'

'It's all strange to me,' Sara commented. 'The river, the valley, your brother—you. I don't quite make you out.'

'Nothing to struggle about,' he shrugged. 'Swing over under that bluff. The channel holds to the east shore along this curve. John and I, huh? Well, of course we look different. He takes after my mother. She was an Italian war bride. Did you know that? Now me, I take after the old man.'

'But there's more to the difference than that?'

'Sure there is. John's older than I am. John's the hard working one. I like to enjoy life. We don't get two tries at life. I like wine, women and song—and the ponies. And I'm not above a whirl at the dice, or a little poker now and again.'

'You said that in the plural!' she teased him.

'Said what?'

'Women—in the plural.'

'Aha! You caught me out,' he said mournfully. 'Sure I chase them. But believe me, Sara, I only chase the ones who want to be caught. They all know the score.'

'And John? What does he do?'

'As I said, Sara, he works hard—spends a great deal of time with his students. John's the smart one. He designed those things we make at the factory, you know. Designed the ICs, designed the machinery to make them, trained the first workers, and turned it all over to me. Beyond that, I don't know—he's a deacon in the church, Selectman in the town. Does a lot in local charities. Let me take the helm now. We'll stop at that island and have lunch.'

Which they did. Robert had brought along three tubs of still-warm Kentucky fried chicken, a few cans of beer for himself, and a quart bottle of lemonade for Sara. After an enjoyable lunch, flavoured by a never-ending series of slightly off-colour anecdotes, they strolled the limits of the island, holding hands. A small cloud eventually covered the sun, and a chill set in. Sara looked up at the western sky with a practised eye.

'We'd better move on,' she called to him. 'There's a storm behind those clouds somewhere.' Robert agreed, and she noted a little regret as they packed up their disposables and cast off. Despite all the warnings, it had been a pleasant afternoon with the wolf.

The clumsy craft ran downstream with only the slight urging of the starboard motor. But a brisk wind, coming in from the north-west, rocked the boat more than Sara had expected.

'After a time she called to him, 'May I ask you a personal question, Robert?'

'Ask away,' he returned. 'I have no secrets from Sara.'

'How come John inherited the farm and everything?'

'Because he's the sober one,' he laughed. 'My father could see that I was as much a hellion as he'd been. So he left John in control. With good reason, mind you! John's gotten me out of a lot of scrapes in my day. Let's face it, Sara—I'm the no-good, and John is Mr Nice, I don't mind admitting it. But I wouldn't trade my fun for all his brains!'

'And it's always been fun, Robert?'

'Well, most of the time. When I have enough money it's fun. But there's a little girl threatening to take me to court right now. And I guess I splurged too much on my last trip down to Atlantic City. I know that they claim down there that the gambling casinos are clean, but those guys that came to talk to me—they were Mr tough Guy himself. I'd swear they were Mafia.'

'Didn't scare you, did they, Robert?'

He looked down at her and laughed. 'I suppose you think, looking at my size, that I'm going to tell you that they didn't? It isn't true. I scare easy. And those guys were enough to scare King Kong. I reached an—an agreement with them! I suppose John would have taken care of them, but not me.'

'You know, you sound a little bit—jealous of John, Robert.'

'Me? Jealous? You could say that I've been envious of him, sure. But to be jealous you have to make an effort. Yeah, I envied John. He had everything I didn't have. But he set me up in this business, you know. If it wasn't for John I wouldn't have the money, the job, my house, my cars—all the things that are important to me. But I don't go off the handle until I'm really peeved. Normally I avoid trouble. Hey, we're almost home, Sara, and it's earlier than I thought. Swing us around into the curent, there's a good girl. Now hold her steady while I drop the anchor.'

She turned the wheel at his direction, and waited for his signal as he released the ratchet on the anchor windlass. As the heavy anchor dropped into the river she gradually reduced power on the engines, and at his command, finally killed them.

'And now what do we do?' she asked, as Robert came back aft, wiping his hands on a cloth.

'Now we have a little friendly fun,' he said. He went into the cabin, and came out a few minutes later with a large inflatable rubber mattress and a couple of blankets. Sara began to get an uneasy feeling as she watched him inflate the mattress from a tiny CO_2 capsule. Then he spread blankets over the mattress.

'Come on, Sara,' he called. 'Let's get with it!'

'Let's get with what?' she gasped, and then shrieked as he swung her up off her feet.

'Let's do it,' he laughed. 'Let's make love. Or whatever they say down by the seaside. Time to pay for your nice boat trip!'

'Don't be silly, Robert!' she yelled, beating on his shoulders with her tiny fists. 'I don't know what kind of a girl you think I am, but——'

'Come off it, Sara,' he laughed, 'we know what kind of a girl you are. John told me all about your little home away from home. And you certainly dressed for the part today, didn't you? Now for crying out loud stop acting like a reluctant virgin and let's get on with it!'

He carried her, still struggling and kicking, over to the mattress, where he threw her down not too gently, and fell on top of her. The fall knocked the breath out of her, but she reached up in a vain attempt to scratch his face. Robert pinned both of her hands in one of his, and laughed again. 'Keep it up, Sara,' he said. 'I love it when you fight. Is this the ploy you use with all your customers?' He leaned forward and kissed her, a brutal contact that bruised her lips and left her in little doubt about her position.

'Wasn't that something?' he asked. He leaned his head down against hers again. In vain Sara tried to bring her knee up at him, but he avoided it by forcing himself between her legs. Then his lips touched hers again, and she bit as hard as she could.

'Hey, damn it!' he cursed. 'It's only a game, Sara. you don't have to take it that far!' He spat out a little blood and then, deadly serious now, seized the bottom of her T-shirt and forced it up over her breasts to her neck.

'Man, is that ever a sight, Sara! Stop wiggling, girl. You know what they say—if rape is inevitable, lie back and enjoy it!' His free hand moved down to the zipper on her slacks and slid it down.

It's no use struggling, Sara, she told herself. Think, girl, think! She lay rigidly still and thought. 'It's about time,' Robert snarled, working the top of her slacks down off her hips. 'If that's the way it's done in the big city, it's a waste of time!'

She looked up at his hovering distorted face. 'Robert,' she said sweetly. 'Robert, I've been talking to Jackie. I need to ask you a question.'

'So ask,' he said disgustedly. 'Get it over. I can't hold back too long.'

'Robert,' she repeated, 'where were you the night that John's wife fell down the stairs and died?'

His face blanched. He cursed under his breath, and moved away from her. 'Why, you little bitch!' he muttered, stunned. But the slight movement was enough to free her. She rolled quickly out from under him, pulling at her slacks with both hands, and ran to the bow. The surprise of her movements put him several steps behind her. As she went by the anchor windlass she released the holding pawl. The anchor line ran out under the pressure of the river current. The clumsy boat danced and swung sideways, and then as the anchor cable came to an end, it snapped the boat up short. Then the anchor broke loose from the river bottom, and the ugly little craft began to stutter-step backwards down the river.

Robert was caught off balance when the anchor line snubbed the boat, and the next movement threw him into the scuppers, where he banged his head against one of the stanchions. It staggered him for only a moment, but that moment was enough. Sara climbed over the near rail, blew him a kiss, and dived into the river.

When she came up, some five yards out in her dive, she rolled over on her back and watched as Robert struggled valiantly to regain control of his craft. Then she rolled over, and using her favourite flutter crawl, made for the dock. A few minutes later both she and Mary were sitting in the Ferrari. She looked down at herself. She was a forlorn, dripping waif, thoroughly soaking all the fine fur seat-covers, and ruining Robert's proud possession. And she loved it! But her clothes, already tight when she had left home, were now clinging to her like a second skin.

Luckily, Robert had left his keys in the car. She started the engine, shifted into drive, and went home. John was standing on the front porch as she drove up. Sara slammed her way out of the car, pushed Mary in front of her, and stomped up the stairs.

'I see you had a good——' he started to say. She smiled at him, her best, most charming smile, as she walked by.

'I had a wonderful time, John. A wonderful time! I don't know when I've enjoyed myself more,' she lied.

'A little too early for swimming, isn't it?'

'Not if you're having fun, John. We were playing a game, and I slipped and fell overboard. But I did so enjoy it!'

She walked by him quickly and squished her way up the stairs to her room. 'Of course I had a wonderful time!' she muttered under her breath. 'What girl wouldn't enjoy it? A wonderful time. Rape on a lovely Sunday afternoon!'

CHAPTER EIGHT

MONDAY morning. The world looked happy, but Sara was miserable. She had wakened early, with the first appearance of the sun. She showered, brushed her teeth and hair, and put on her old green kimono, all the time muttering under her breath. All she could think about was the terrible night which had brought an end to a horrible day.

At least one thing was clear, she told herself. From here on it would have to be the basic old Sara-type. No more imitations of sweet little girls in love! They would have to learn to take her as she was, warts and all. *He* would have to learn to take her! That sounded better, didn't it? She repeated the question to Mary, who politely ignored the subject, and butted Sara towards the door with her big head.

'Don't push!' Sara snarled. Her dog, long accustomed to early morning grouches, licked her hand. 'That's all everybody in this house is interested in,' Sara snapped. 'Eating! And most of the time they think that I'm on the menu! Come on!'

She grumbled her way downstairs, and through the kitchen door, limping because she had lost a slipper in transit. She had come down early, hoping to rescue the day with a cup of coffee before the family got up, but her plan was instantly ruined. John was already sitting at the kitchen table. He took one look at the storm clouds riding above her eyebrows and ducked behind the morning paper. She stalked over to the sink and glared out the window. 'I dare you to say something,' she growled. 'I just double dare you!'

He lowered the paper so that his eyes could be seen above its top. 'Good morning?' he proposed.

'Don't talk to me,' she snapped. 'your behaviour was

terrible—like an animal! And anyway, I never talk to anybody in the morning until I've had my coffee!'

He laid the paper aside, reached for the pot, and poured her a mug of the black steaming liquid. Sara summoned up her fiercest stare, slammed herself down in the chair farthest from him, and clenched her teeth. He picked up his paper again and hid behind it. She sipped at the coffee, mentally composing all the cold and cutting things she would say when her coffee was finished.

'Why did you do it?' she demanded, her voice husky with emotion.

'You mean why did I follow you upstairs to your room? Because I wanted to, that's why.'

'And then you slammed the door so hard that everybody in the house knew you were in my room! You're a beast, that's what you are. What do you think Mrs Emory is thinking this morning?' Her voice rose in outrage.

'Who cares?' he snarled back. 'You spent half the day with Robert, dressed in your wet seduction suit. What did you expect me to say? Something like "How lovely your breasts look in your wet T-shirt, Sara." Or would you have preferred something on the order of "And that's a lovely outfit you're almost wearing, Sara." Would that have suited you better?'

'There was nothing wrong with my clothes,' she snarled back, knowing it was a lie. 'And they fitted me fine. You had no need to call it a harlot suit, did you? And then to go and rip my T-shirt off! You're a monster! You ought to be confined!'

John had the grace to put his paper down. There was a contrite look on his face, but his eyes were still showering sparks. 'I admit that I may have carried things too far, Sara, and I apologise. It was not a harlot suit. And I shouldn't have ripped your T-shirt. I have a very bad temper, and you made me more angry than I've ever been in my life!'

'And that gave you the right to—to maul me! And to kiss me?' she raved.

'I can explain that, Sara,' he snorted. 'How was I to know you were wearing—so little under that shirt? When it accidentally—yes, accidentally—ripped off, I thought it might be better to kiss you rather than to stand there with my mouth open, half-witted, just staring at you!' he leaned forward across the table. 'Why don't you understand, Sara? There you were, standing as if you had no idea in the world what effect you have on a man. There's—so much of you—and in such a lovely shape, Sara. A man would have to be blind and ninety years old not to want to grab!'

'Well, I'm not a grab bag,' she said flatly, 'and I don't make a practice of entertaining men in my bedroom. You'd better learn, Mr Englewood, that if you expect me to stay here for six months, to your benefit, you're going to have to keep your hands to yourself. Just because Mary likes you doesn't mean that you have a free access to either me or my bedroom. You hear me?'

'How could I not hear you?' he asked. 'Everyone in the house could have heard!' He put his elbows on the table and rested his chin on the palms of his hands.

'Why were you so mad?' she asked. 'Because I went out with Robert? I asked your permission, you remember?'

'Yes, I remember. Yes, I was angry with you—not because you went out with Robert, but because you enjoyed it so much! I hadn't expected that. I do give you some credit. You did come back with all your clothes on, and that's not the normal thing when Robert takes a girl out. But you enjoyed it so much! That's what made me so damn angry!'

Sara leaned across the table and touched his arm. 'Poor John,' she half whispered. 'Poor troubled John. And am I such a burden to you? I really didn't enjoy it at all, you know. You must know that?'

He stared at her, a whole host of expressions fleeting across his face. Then he scraped back his chair and walked towards the door. 'And I don't need your pity,

Sara. That's the last thing I would want!' The door swung shut behind him, and all the horizons of Sara's world collapsed.

Her school trip with Jackie was made without incident. On her way home she noticed that there were more pickets outside the plant, and that they were getting noisier. At the house, Mrs Emory was busy waxing the kitchen floor, so Sara and Mary went off for a walk. When they returned, wrestling with each other in the hall, Mrs Emory came out of the kitchen.

'Telephone for you, Sara,' she said from the doorway. 'Same man been calling you all the morning. He wouldn't say a word when I told him you weren't in—just left his number and hung up.'

Sara pushed the dog away from her, rose gracefully to her feet, and went down the hall to the loveseat by the telephone.

'I don't see why you treat that animal as if she was a human being,' Mrs Emory complained, 'and for goodness' sakes, girl, pull down your blouse! There's more of you showing than is decent!' There was a twinkle in the housekeeper's eye that effectively dispelled the sting of the words. Sara detoured from the direct line to the telephone long enough to kiss Emma on her cheek, at which Mrs Emory turned several shades of red and dashed for the kitchen, declaring, 'Well, I do declare!'

Sara accomplished some emergency rearrangement of her clothes and then picked up the receiver. Not to her surprise she heard the raspy voice of Harry Burton, the retired labour organiser from Point Judith. 'Oh, Harry!' she exclaimed with delight, 'how in the world did you get here so quickly? Where are you? When can I see you?'

'One question at a time, Sara,' he replied. 'Did you ever hear of the invention of the aeroplane. I'm down here in Springfield, about twenty minutes from where you are I'll be staying at the Mohawk Motel, on Route Five, just west of Deerfield. Know where it is?'

'No, Harry, I don't, but I'm sure I can find it. Shall I come right away?'

'No, Sara baby. I've been talking with the people of Local 621. We'll meet this afternoon up at that motel. I see you stirred up a fuss, as usual. Now, there's a coffee shop at the motel. On Wednesday morning I'll be there with another guy. It'll be the man you want to talk to, baby. He's sceptical, but willing to listen. Okay?'

'Certainly, Harry. It's so good of you to come and help. So good, Harry.'

'Good hell,' he rasped. 'You call—I come. Ain't you the girl that gave me the kiss of life two years ago? You called in a marker, kid. I owe you a lot more. What time can you come?'

'Would nine o'clock do? I could come over just as soon as I take my son to school.'

'Sara,' he shouted, 'is there something wrong with this connection? You did say right after you take *what* son to school?'

'Oh dear, I made a mistake, Harry,' she muttered into the telephone.

'Yeah—but you only been gone from the Point for two weeks, Sara. That kind of mistake still takes nine months!'

'Honestly, Harry,' she sighed, 'It was a slip of the tongue. I have to take a little boy to school. Right after that I'll be over.'

'Okay, Sara, that will be fine. Oh, before I forget— you did tell me when you called that you had a piece of the action at this plant. How big a piece, baby?'

'I have voting control of fifteen per cent of the outstanding shares, Harry.' She could hear voices in the background as Harry consulted with someone else. Then he returned to the line.

'That's fine, Sara. You can come on Wednesday. And Sara? None of this little girl stuff. Put on your grown-up bib and tucker.'

'Okay, Harry,' she laughed. 'Nine o'clock, dressed elderly, and you'll spring for the coffee?' He was laughing uproariously as he severed the connection.

That night when she went with Jackie for his bath ritual, John was missing. When the little boy had dropped off to sleep Sara gathered up her sewing and went hesitantly downstairs. She went into the deserted sitting room feeling down in the mouth, but arranged her cushions as always at the foot of John's chair. She was daydreaming, watching the blue-tipped flames in the fireplace, when he came in. He was no longer in pinstripes, she noticed. His tan slacks and shirt were topped off with a buckskin sports coat, which he took off and dropped on the coffee table.

'Tough day at the office,' he commented. 'Faculty meeting. It's almost impossible to get sixteen Ph.D.s to listen while someone else talks. Still angry with me, Sara?' She moved over slightly as he sank into his chair, then scrambled up to fetch him a footstool. He smiled gratefully as she coiled herself down on her cushions again.

'No, I'm not mad at you, John. I seem to be forever saying that to you, don't I? Did you have supper?'

'I had a ham sandwich and a bottle of beer. That's enough to go on.'

'I could get you something more,' she offered, but he dropped a hand on her shoulder and settled her back down again. 'Later Sara, later. Let's just sit and relax.' She leaned back against his chair, her left arm resting on his knee. His fingers toyed with her loosened hair.

'This is more like it. A nice comfortable home, and a beautiful girl to come home to,' he mused. 'Sara, do you remember yesterday when I made those stupid remarks about your clothes, did you mean what you said?'

'Mean what, John?'

'You said that if I were your husband I wouldn't have to beat you, just command you. Did you mean that, Sara?'

'You mean if I *had* a husband? Well, certainly I would expect him to command me.'

'And you would obey him?'

'We're only talking hypothetically, John. I've never had a husband. But Mamma always told me that a man should be master in his own home, and the woman of his house should go along with him, unless it was a matter of the greatest principle or importance. So yes, I guess if I loved a man enough to marry him I would certainly let him command me—some of the time.'

She answered him lightly, her mind really surrounded by the dream world of fire and warmth and his presence. His voice penetrated the haze in a soothing, comforting way that left Sara at peace with her world. His hand continued to gently ruffle her hair, and she felt a curious longing that he might never stop.

'It all takes me back a long way,' he said, after several minutes of contemplation. 'It *is* peaceful here, isn't it?'

'You must have loved and missed her a good deal,' she answered sympathetically.

'Missed who?'

'Your wife, of course.'

'Missed Elena? You must be out of your mind, Sara!' She squirmed completely round to look at him, surprise evident on her face.

'But John——' she started to say.

'Don't paint castles in the air. Marrying Elena was like getting a surprise Christmas present. When I finally got her unwrapped I found I'd married a nymphomaniac!'

'But you must have loved her a little. And then there's Jackie.'

'Yes, I suppose I did love her once. But that lasted about three months. As for Jackie—well, she always maintained that he was her second greatest mistake. We were both drunk that night!'

'Did you hate her for that?' asked Sara.

'No, I never hated her. There was never any hate involved, except for that night. I don't know what you've heard, Sara. I've never wanted to talk about it before. My lovely wife was about to leave me. She was running off with another man. But she was dead drunk, and fell down the stairs and broke her neck! How's that for retribution, Sara?'

'And you hated her for that?'

'I told you, I never hated her at all. It was a sickness. I felt sorry for her, I despised the things she did, but I never hated her. No.' John leaned forward and cupped her face between his hands. 'There was someone here that night she died, Sara—the man she was running off with. Him I hate. No, not because he was stealing Elena—God knows she was never mine to be stolen. I hate him because he left that little kid alone in the dark of night, crying over her dead body. And believe me, if I ever find out who it was, I'll kill the bastard!'

'Please, John! You're hurting me!' Sara exclaimed.

He dropped his hands immediately, looking flustered. He beat one hard fist into the palm of his other hand. 'I'm sorry, Sara,' he apologised. 'I never mean to hurt you, but I always seem to end up doing just that. But when I think of—come on, Sara, let's go and take a walk!'

On Wednesday morning Sara woke up late. Jackie had already clattered downstairs. She jumped out of bed and went to the window. The sun was shining brightly again. The scent of lilacs was fading as the blossoms dropped, to be replaced by the fragrance of apple. She took eight deep breaths, meaning to follow her morning exercise routine, but a glance at the clock put an end to that. She hurried through her shower, and dodged out before her hair became really wet. She brushed her hair quickly, fastening it up again in the coronets which added years to her appearance. She chose a simple blue silk dress for the day, a high-necked collarless dress with pleated skirt. She added her only pair of high heels, and bypassed her contact lenses in favour of the hornrimmed glasses. She added only a touch of lipstick, but did touch her throat and wrists with a drop of Heather, her favourite perfume.

When she came downstairs Mrs Emory was standing

in the kitchen door, and Jackie was hopping up and down by the front door.

'Come on, Sara,' the little boy wailed, 'we'll be late!'

'Nobody goes out of my house without breakfast,' Mrs Emory declared. 'And what kind of a disguise is this in aid of, Sara? Trying to catch the eye of the veterans of foreign wars?'

'Just a cup of coffee and a piece of toast,' Sara pleaded. 'We really shall be late. Jackie will be mad at me, and I can't afford to lose this job. It's my only source of income these days.'

Mrs Emory disappeared into the kitchen, only to have her place taken at the door by John. He was casually dressed, in denims and a light blue open shirt. He handed Sara the cup of coffee he was carrying. 'Already saucered and blowed.' he said. 'What's this about income? You need money, Sara?'

'I'm broke,' she chuckled, sipping thirstily at the cooled coffee. 'Jackie's paying me, you know—a nickel a week. And that's all the income I have.'

'We can do——' John started to say, but was interrupted by Mrs Emory.

'Two pieces of toast, dearie,' the housekeeper said. 'And you'd better be on your way. And John, you've had a telephone call from the Town Clerk. He says you must bring copies of both blood tests with you. Give me the cup if it's empty, Sara.'

Sara stuffed one piece of toast in her mouth, thrust the coffee cup into Emma's hand, and ran for the door. As she went out she could see Jackie and Mary both sitting in the car, and it struck her for the first time that she hadn't seen her dog at all that morning!

Mrs Emory closed the front door behind Sara, shaking her head. 'I don't understand it,' she mumbled to herself. 'The only thing you need a blood test for in Massachusetts is a marriage licence.'

'What's nagging me, young man,' Sara mumbled through the toast, 'is how come you got *my* dog?'

'She came into my room last night, when I was

having a bad dream. She slept by my bed,' the boy answered. 'Can't she be my dog too?'

'Say, I don't know about that. A guard dog isn't supposed to make friends with people—they get to be pets that way. But Mary's getting to be a little old for guarding anyway, so I guess I could make an exception.'

'You don't need no guard dog, Sara,' he piped up. 'You got me and Daddy to guard you now, don't you?'

'What a lovely thought,' Sara chuckled. 'Do you suppose you daddy would lie down by my bed at night and guard me?'

'Sara, you're funny,' he replied in a reprimanding voice. 'Daddies don't lie on the floor all night. They get in the bed, like Daddy did the other night. You and him in the bed together—gee, that was funny!'

Out of the mouths of babes, Sara thought as she blushed to the roots of her hair. 'I didn't see anything funny about it, you little rascal,' she retorted. 'I don't have a big bed, and your daddy snores—and you'd better not say another word about *that*, little wise guy! How come you saw all this?'

'I got up for a glass of water,' he said.

'Well, button your lip, smarty pants,' she growled.

'Yes, Mommy,' he said gravely, then burst out laughing.

Sara was still nibbling her lip over this latest calamity in a long line of calamities, when she pulled up in front of the Mohawk Motel. She climbed out of the car, rearranged her skirt, patted her hair, and whistled Mary out of the back seat. With one hand on the dog's leash she strolled into the semi-darkness of the coffee shop. She stopped just inside the door to allow her eyes to adjust to the light. As she stood there, one of the waiters came over to her.

'No dogs allowed in here, lady.,' he told her.

'No? She's my seeing eye dog,' Sara lied as prettily as she knew how.

'Don't look like no seeing eye dog to me,' he retorted.

'Well, in that case why don't you take her outside?'

Sara suggested. The waiter moved a step closer, and Mary bared her teeth and growled.

'Hey, Sara,' a voice called from the other side of the room. 'Over here!' In the distance she could barely make out Harry Burton and three other burly white-haired men, sitting at a table.

'You with them guys?' the waiter asked in surprise. Then he looked at Mary again. 'Okay,' he said, 'take your seeing eye dog with you.'

'Thank you very much,' Sara replied. The waiter watched as she walked by, but she knew he was looking at her high-heeled walk, not at her dog. She stopped halfway and turned around. 'I just can't help it, you know,' she said. 'I'm built that way!' The waiter flushed and scurried behind the bar.

Harry stood up to welcome her as she came over to the table. 'Hi, Sara baby!' he roared, and kissed her on the forehead.

'Oh, Harry,' she sighed as she went into his arms and hugged him, 'can't you ever talk softer than a force ten gale?'

'Nope. No reason to,' he laughed. 'Sit down here, Sara.' He offered her the seat he had just vacated. 'This is the guy you wanted to meet, Sara—Skip Evans. Skip, this is Susan Anderson—Sara we call her.'

The man looked to be about fifty, about six feet tall, and several yards wide. The hand he offered was three times the size of Sara's. Her little paw seemed to disappear when he engulfed it. Mary nosed up to the table and growled. Evans smiled at the dog and the girl, and released the hand.

'She gives you a time-limit for hand-holding?' he asked. His voice was a raspy bariton, full of authority.

'Yes,' Sara replied. 'She's not a pet.'

'I can see that,' he said. 'Neither are you, are you?'

She dimpled an acknowledgement. He sat down, still studying her. She looked enquiringly at the other two men. 'You don't need to know them,' Skip Evans told her. 'They're from the strike committee. It's a tricky business, us talking to someone from management. They're just here to listen.'

Sara nodded to them all, then reached into her purse for the financial reports that Packy Muldoon had analysed for her. 'Now then, Mr Evans——'

'Skip,' he insisted.

'All right—Skip. I'm not really from management. I saw the girl who was burned. I've met the man who says he's the President. I talked to some of the people on the picket line. I am, at least temporarily, a stockholder. There hasn't been a dividend paid in two years, and the union has had only one three per cent raise in two years. I've read these silly statements, and had them analysed. Now the question is, what can we do about all this, you and I?'

'The plant is booming,' he returned. 'Two shifts going for the past four years. For a girl who's only been in the area for a couple of weeks you've been pretty busy. I like that.' He raised his coffee cup, scrutinising her over its rim. 'What we have got is absentee management,' he continued. 'He sits in his office and never stirs. He hasn't the slightest idea about what's going on. The plant is being run by his secretaries and his cronies. And nobody listens when we file a grievance.'

'So what we need is a new management team? You think that's all?'

'It would be a big help.' He turned to the other two men and raised his eyebrows. They both nodded in agreement.

'Miss Anderson—Sara,' he said, 'We know a lawyer. According to the by-laws of the company, it takes ten per cent of the stock votes to call a special meeting of the board of directors. The union would be at the table. We hold three per cent of the stock ourselves. We could force a discussion of the troubles—but then what? The two Englewood brothers own over eighty per cent of the stock between them.'

'If we could arrange this meeting,' said Sara, 'I think perhaps I could come up with something. But before we see this lawyer, I missed breakfast. And I have another problem I want to talk to you about.'

'Okay, you guys, you can go back to the picket line,' Skip Evans said. His two compatriots, without having said a word, got up, nodded cheerfully to Sara, and walked out. Harry got up too and walked over to the counter. 'Ham and eggs for three,' he roared.

'Make that for four,' Sara called. 'Mary hasn't eaten either.'

'Your dog eats ham and eggs?' Skip asked.

Sara nodded. 'But only when she can't get steak and eggs,' she told him. 'Mary is a high-class eater.'

'Funny name, Mary,' he commented, making small talk until the breakfast arrived.

'Like mine,' Sara rejoined. 'She's registered in the American Kennel Club as Duchess Maria Henrietta von Furstenburg. I couldn't quite hack that, so—Mary.'

Harry arrived with more coffee. The waiter followed with four separate plates of ham and eggs. He glowered when Sara slipped one of the plates down to the floor. The two older men at the table stared hard at him, and he walked away without speaking. Sara gave Mary the hand signal to eat.

'Dig or talk?' Skip asked.

'Both,' Sara replied. She picked up her fork and began to do justice to the meal. 'Hard to ruin ham and eggs,' she added as she swallowed her third forkful. 'Even in the hospital cafeteria, where they really know how to murder food!'

'Ah, that,' Skip replied as he too dug in. 'Harry says you're a nurse. You don't look it—too small, too cute!'

'Short,' she corrected him automatically. 'And what would your wife think about that?'

He acknowledged the stab.

'Are your hypodermic needles as sharp as your tongue, little miss?' he enquired.

'Best nurse in all of Point Judith,' Harry added, without indication that she was the *only* nurse in Point Judith.

'The other problem I want to talk about is theft, Skip,' Sara said after she had wiped some of the dripping egg from her chin.

He put his fork down beside his plate and stared at her. 'You sure you want to talk about that?' he asked.

'I'm sure. Very sure,' she retorted.

'So talk,' he said guardedly.

'What these statements really say, Skip, is that there's either a very big pile of spoiled chips at the factory, or somebody is taking the stuff out of the warehouse by the back door. And maybe somebody pretty high up is dipping into the till.' She stopped to consider her own statements, tapping her fingers on the pamphlets on the table. 'Or all three,' she concluded.

Skip was giving her his full attention. He pushed his unfinished plate to one side. His eyes had become hard. 'We have less than one-tenth of one per cent spoilage,' he said softly. 'So what else?'

'Harry,' said Sara, 'why don't you go take a walk for a minute or two?'

'Take a walk, baby?' he asked. 'Why would I want to take a walk? I ain't finished my breakfast.'

'Yes, you have, Harry. Take a walk. I love you very much, you old fraud, but in Massachusetts two is a conversation, three is a conspiracy.' Harry got up, laughing, and walked to the door. Sara looked back at Skip.

'I've been told,' she said, 'that the plant has no security guards, and only one night watchman. I've been told that the town has only three policemen, and that if you want a cop at night you have to call one of them at their homes. If you can find them.'

'You've been told right, little lady. Are you suggesting that the union is stealing goods?'

'No, Skip. But there's no way I can get dividends, or you can get a raise, until we see that the company makes a profit. Right?'

'Possibly,' he said disgustedly. 'And then?'

'You're a big man, Mr Evans.'

'Yes?'

'And I wouldn't be surprised but what you've got

four or five big friends?'

'Wouldn't be surprised.'

'What I would like to do,' she continued, 'is to have somebody watch the plant every night for the next ten days. I have a suspicion that a truck will appear on one of those nights, and someone will open the warehouse door for them, and that they'll load up with half of our profits.'

'You realise what you are saying? It takes a big organisation to sell these chips on the black market. You're talking Mafia.'

'I'm talking survival,' she said bitterly. 'The plant is on the edge of going under. You want that?'

'No!' he snorted. 'So somebody watches, and somebody sees this truck. And then what? We call the cops and they arrive the week after next?'

'No. What I had in mind is that we find out who it is in the plant who's opening the door.'

'And then we call the police?'

Sara looked at him carefully before she answered. 'No,' she replied. 'You know, Skip, I'm really not a nice girl at all. What I want is for this fellow, or these fellows, to have a very sudden accident that might discourage them. They might break an arm. But not a leg, mind you. They might want to leave town very quickly.'

The big man was laughing. She watched, trying to decide whether it was with her or at her. Finally he got himself under control. 'I pity the man who marries you, little lady,' he said. 'What you're saying is that our union should take on the Mafia. Okay—we'll do it.' He reached across the table and touched her hand for a fleeting second. 'You're a lovely creature, Susan Anderson. Thank God I'm not your enemy. Let's go see that lawyer!'

They both stood up, and Harry, seeing them move, came to join them. As a result, Sara went out into the sunlight with a tall husky elderly gentleman on either side of her. Outside the door Harry recalled a couple of his better one-liners. They stood laughing at each other until Harry had to make his goodbyes. With her usual enthusiasm Sara reached up on tiptoes and gave him a kiss and a hearty hug. What with the laughter, the enjoyment of the moment, and the bright sun in her eyes, she failed entirely to see the heavy Chrysler that had slowed at the side of the road when they appeared. Nor did she hear its driver cursing as he floored the gas pedal and screeched the vehicle out of the area.

Their meeting with the lawyer took less than an hour.

'I should be able to file notice with the secretary by one o'clock today,' that worthy said. 'Notice will be in the hands of the principal stockholders by five tonight. The agenda, as I understand it, is to be a discussion of plant security, an outside audit of all funds and accounts, and the election of new officers.'

'That's about it,' Sara agreed. Skip looked at her in some puzzlement. 'Outside audit?' he asked. 'You know something I don't know?'

'Yes,' said Sara, and left them both to stare after her as she jauntily clicked her way out of the office, swaying gracefully on her high heels. She still had time to spare before Jackie was to be picked up, so she combed the few shops in town for a dress that had only a few requirements placed upon it. 'It needs to be white, demure, simple, and sexy!' she told herself fiercely. And when she found it she paid not the least notice to the price tag, but gladly cashed three of her travellers cheques to pay for it.

She was home some time before John was due. She took her new dress out of its wrapping and held it up in front of her. 'If this doesn't stir his stumps,' she told herself, 'then he's made out of wood entirely!' She slipped the dress on and waltzed around the room, humming a tune. Mrs Emory, who was cleaning the bathroom, came to the door.

'Nice to hear somebody in this house singing,' the housekeeper commented. 'It's like a tomb around here when you're not in the house, Sara. Why, that dress looks darling! New?'

'Yes, just bought,' Sara carolled. 'Look at me, Emma!' She hurled herself around the room for one more circuit. 'Look at me! I've spent my last dollar just to entertain a man!'

'We all do that,' Mrs Emory chuckled. 'But you've missed the boat, my dear. John won't be home tonight. He called in this afternoon, mad as a wet hen—said he had to go up to Boston on business and won't be back until tomorrow night. Little bit low in the bosom there, isn't it?' and she disappeared into the bathroom again.

'Damn! Damn! Damn!' Sara muttered. 'Why doesn't something go right for a change!' And then, staring into the mirror, 'Do you suppose there's too much for me showing? Maybe I should take a tuck?' But the mirror refused to answer. There were tears in her eyes as she put the new dress back on a hanger and returned it to the wardrobe. Instead of a princess, she thought, I might as well play the pauper. So she pulled out one of the little A-line dresses and slipped it over her head. As she walked to the door she was very careful not to look in the mirror.

She wandered downstairs to offer her help in the kitchen, only to be refused by Mrs Emory. 'New England boiled dinner,' Emma announced. 'Everything is in the pot.'

Sara ate with Jackie and Emma in the kitchen rather than the dining room, then paced the veranda until dusk. At ten o'clock the telephone rang. She rushed into the hall to answer.

'Sara?' the heavy male voice said, 'this is Evans—Skip Evans. Bingo?'

'Somebody came tonight?' she gasped.

'A little sports van, right after dark—two hoods from Springfield. One of them was carrying a piece.'

'You stopped the truck? What was he carrying?'

'A piece, Sara—a 38-calibre pistol. Yeah, we stopped the truck. Things got a little confused then. They'd loaded five thousand units from the warehouse. Three men in the warehouse, all kids from the shipping room. All nice and legal. They had a shipping ticket, all signed and legal. Guess who signed it?'

'I don't have to guess,' she sighed, 'Robert Englewood! What did you do?'

'The truck drivers gave us a little lip. They thought we were hijacking their shipment. One of them has a broken nose, and the other managed somehow to break his arm—he was the guy with the gun. Wait'll they get back to Springfield, Sara. There's going to be hell to pay. There has to be a fix involved in all this, and when the Springfield Capo finds out his shipment came unglued the rockets will go up!'

'And the kids from the shipping room?'

'Nothing we could do. We scared hell out of them and told them to keep their noses clean in the future. And that's the story. Everything else okay, Sara?'

'Yes,' she said, and hung up. Snoopy Sara, she told herself. Nosey Sara, minding everybody's business. Why did it matter that something was going on at the plant? If John knew, would he want anybody hurt because of it? If only John would come home! She slipped on a jacket and went back out to her pacing on the veranda. Every set of lights that sparkled on the highway might be John, coming back!

She was feeling magnificently sorry for herself when, at midnight, John had not come, but the telephone rang. She slammed her way back into the house, tripping over Mary in her haste. The minute she heard the voice her climbing spirits nosedived.

'What in the world do you want, Robert?' she groaned. 'Hurry up—I'm waiting for a call from John.'

'Sara,' he shouted, 'I have to see you. I *must* see you—right now! It's a matter of life and death!'

'Why the devil should I want to see you,' she snarled. 'After the way you treated me on Sunday I'd think you——'

'Sara,' he interrupted, 'to hell with Sunday! If you want me to kiss your foot I'll do it, but I can't wait. I have to see you before eight o'clock in the morning. Please, Sara—it's important. Very important.'

'All right,' she sighed, 'if you must. Come now. And come prepared to behave yourself. Mary will be with me.'

'Right,' he answered. 'Right away.'

CHAPTER NINE

THE old house creaked in all its joints as the wind picked up and rattled its corners. Sara went into the sitting room, commanding Mary to lie down on the rug in the hall, just outside the sitting room door. She cleared the desk top, built up the fire, and stood waiting. Promptly at twelve-thirty the doorbell rang. She took one more look around the room, and shivered. 'Enter the Villain, Stage Left,' she told herself, and went to open the door. Robert followed her back into the sitting room. Mary growled as he passed, but lay still. He took a seat on the sofa, and Sara promptly sat down in the armchair farthest from him.

'Not offering me a drink, Sara?' he asked.

'I don't think so. We don't have any hemlock available. Now, it's late. Perhaps you could come directly to this urgent life-or-death business you spoke about?'

Robert rubbed his hands together, as if to warm them before the fire. In this better light she could see that his face was pale, his usually perfect hair dishevelled. He walked over to the drinks cabinet and helped himself to a double Scotch, which he downed with one gulp.

'Something has gone wrong, Sara,' he began, 'and I don't want John to get in any trouble. I can take care of the matter myself, providing I could have control of your voting rights in the corporation. It would not be any trouble for you, Sara. You always said you knew nothing about business. All you have to do is sign this proxy form—and—well, I know you care for John, Sara, and would want to help him. I do too. Just one signature, and I'll be able——'

She held up her hand. 'Stop babbling, Robert. You know as well as I do that it's not for John. It's for your own neck you're concerned. You want my help?

Start from the beginning, and for once in your life be honest!'

He went back to the drinks cabinet and fortified himself with a second double. 'You're right, Sara, of course.' He settled down on the sofa again and twirled his glass in the firelight.

'It all started about two years ago,' he said. 'I got myself over a barrel, what with the ponies and the gambling tables. I finally had to go to a loan shark. And then it got worse. I couldn't pay off the loan shark. And that's dangerous. So I arranged a—a barter situation with them. As long as I had Aunt Lucinda's proxy, and my own stock, there was no problem. But now things have changed. There's a call out for a stockholders' meeting. Somebody wants an audit, and a new election of officers. And tonight there was an—interruption in our delivery schedule. And some people—some people have told me it has to be corrected. They've given me until eight o'clock tomorrow to regain absolute control over the corporation.'

'Or else?'

'Yes. There's always an "or else." They've made me an offer I can't refuse.'

'Are you scared, Robert?' she asked drily.

'My God, woman, what are you saying? Scared? I'm petrified! they aren't talking about a friendly warning, or a court summons or something. They're talking about a broken leg—if I'm lucky.'

'Why did you let yourself get into such a mess in the first place?' she asked.

'You don't understand, do you, Sara? All you goody-goody people. Damn it, you don't let yourself—it just happens!'

'So why don't you just sell your stock in the company, Robert, or your cars, or your boat? You could make a pretty penny on them. Or that wonderful house?'

'But—but, Sara,' he exclaimed. 'Please, Sara! This

company doesn't mean a thing to you, does it? But with me it's different. Don't you understand, Sara? This job, this house, those cars, that boat—all that is *me*, Sara. They're not just possessions, they're *me*! If I lost them, I'll have lost all I am! Oh sure, John would be all right without all that—he'd just go off in a corner and invent something. But I can't do that—I won't do that! I like my life, Sara, and—sign the proxy, Sara. Sign the proxy.'

'Why, Robert? So you can go on dipping your fingers in the till, peddling goods on the black market, living the high life on John's ideas? Well, what you said is true. I don't give a damn about the company, or about your money problems. If that's all it was, Robert, I would sign your proxy form in a second. But that isn't all, Robert. You'd better have another drink.'

He looked at her, stunned, then walked over to replenish his glass. He started back towards her, changed his mind, downed the drink he had just poured, and made himself another.

'Now, Robert, listen to me. I said it once, I'll say it again. I don't give a hoot about the company, or your embezzlements, or your Mafia deals. I'd sign your proxy in a minute, just because you're John's brother. But what bothers me, Robert, is what happened in this house the night Elena died. You remember that night? And what happened to Jackie? I've talked a great deal with Jackie during the last two weeks. And you know something? If you were drowning I wouldn't throw you a rope, you miserable worm!' Her voice was coloured with loathing. It struck him like a blow in the face.

She could see his colour change as he struggled to express himself. His fists clenched and he began to breathe faster. Suddenly Sara was struck by the precarious nature of her own position. To all practical purposes she was alone in the house with this man. And even a rat, pushed into a corner, would attack!

Robert got up and began to pace up and down the room. 'I hear you, Sara,' he said between clenched teeth. 'It's all a game with you, isn't it, Sara? Nosey Parker

Anderson. I knew it was you who arranged for the stockholders' meeting, Sara. I knew.' He walked by her chair, and she managed to shrink away from him. 'Just a little busybody, licking up to sweet brother John. I knew it was all you, you little bitch!' And before she could react he had slammed the door to the sitting room.

He came back and stood in front of her. 'And now, little Sara. We have your playmate on the outside, and you on the inside,' he gloated. 'Want to change your mind?'

She shook her head. 'Not now. Not never, Robert.'

He leaned over her and barricaded her in the chair by placing one of his hands on each chair arm. 'You think you can upset my whole applecart, Sara? Well, let me tell you something—it'll take more than a ten-dollar callgirl to do that! You may not vote my way, little girl, but I'm sure going to spoil you for sweet honest John. Before this night is over I'm going to have you, baby— the hard way. Right here! Right now!'

He reached out for her. She pushed back against the chair, upsetting it, and spilling herself out on the floor behind it. One of her shoulders crashed into the coffee table, sending a spear of pain through her, and Robert came around the chair. 'Mary,' Sara yelled. 'Mary! Help!' She scrambled away from him, but his heavy fist managed to make contact with the corner of her eye, knocking her back over the desk and on to the floor again. She struggled to get free from the office chair behind the desk, pushing it in his way just soon enough to trip him. He fell forward, but one outstretched hand managed to catch her dress at the neck. As she rolled away the dress ripped, and one of his fingernails traced a bloody line from her throat to her stomach.

A tremendous thud came from the door, as eighty pounds of enraged animal threw itself at the heavy door and its ancient latch. Robert got up again, and Sara ran around the desk. She threw a lamp stand into his path, but he managed to dodge it. She backed fearfully into the corner. The pounding at the door continued. He came at her a vicious grin on his face. It transformed him into a twisted and distorted imitation of man wrapped in dark passions. He grabbed her by both naked shoulders, so tightly that his fingernails bit into her flesh.

'Well, little girl,' he laughed, 'in the corner now, and no place to run?' He squeezed harder, then shook her until her neck almost snapped. She screamed again. Robert freed one hand and slapped her heavily on each cheek. The hammering at the door continued. He seized a handful of her hair and used it to draw her to him. She tried to knee him in the groin, but he saw it coming and threw her, off balance, into the wall. She slid to the floor, almost unconscious. Once again he pulled her up, his heavy signet ring scratching her back as he did so. Sara felt unable to resist any more. She leaned against him, whimpering in pain. The sound added to his fury. Beyond all control, he picked her up and threw her down on the sofa.

'Now you can show me all the ways it's done in the big city,' he muttered. One of his rough hands tortured her breast as the other ripped at her bikini briefs. 'Come on,' he taunted. 'I'll even pay you. Show me how they do it in the big city!'

He started to lower his weight on to her, pressing against her with a knee, forcing himself between her thighs. She screamed again, and at that moment a hand turned the knob on the door, and the huge dog scrabbled into the room at full speed, saliva dripping from her mouth, her great fangs poised.

Robert heard the noise and rolled off Sara on to the floor. He tried to run before his legs were under him, but the dog had already taken him by the shoulder, shaking and worrying him, teeth dug in deep through his jacket. Flat on the floor, whimpering himself now, he dug his heels in and managed to pull himself to the wall.

'What the hell is going on here?' The deep voice from the doorway managed to penetrate through the fog of Sara's brain. Somewhere in the room a female voice was screaming. Short, dry-throated screams they were, that gradually sank to the level of sobs, and then faded out. John's strong arms came gently around her and squeezed her into a haven of safety. Her long hair had fallen down, and swathed her face and shoulders like a veil. The bruises and blood were hidden. She pressed closer to him, totally oblivious to the fact that she was naked.

'For God's sake,' John said coldly, 'call off your damn dog. Are you trying to kill him?'

'Yes!' she screamed into his shirt front. He pushed her away and tried to look into her eyes. She ducked her head against his chest, hiding.

'Mary,' he yelled, 'sit!'

The dog paid him no attention. Robert had pulled himself up to a sitting position against the wall. He sat there, frozen in terror, as the big dog worried his shoulder. John made a tentative move, as if not sure which of them needed his attention first. As he debated, he stripped off his jacket and wrapped it around Sara's shivering shoulders. 'Call off the dog!' he ordered her again.

She took one step away from him, and clumsily pushed her battered arms into the sleeves of the coat. She fumbled with the buttons, and the coat, which barely reached a couple of inches past his waist, swung heavily down below her knees.

'Call off your damn dog!' he shouted at her. He moved forward and stretched a restraining hand towards Mary. The dog released the shoulder grip and turned her head around towards, him, growling.

'Mary!' she called. The dog looked at her. Her voice would not come. She gave the hand signal to heel. The dog paused, looked back at Robert with bared fangs, then gradually backed off until she stood at Sara's feet. Sara's legs were too weak to hold her. She crumpled to the floor, wrapping her arms around the panting animal, pressing her face into the rough fur of Mary's foreleg.

As soon as he saw Sara's arms go around the dog, Robert scrambled to his feet. The marks of panic and fear flashed from his face. He brushed off the sleeve of his jacket, but did not look at his brother.

'Well?' John stared at Robert. His back was to Sara.

'The bitch tried to proposition me,' Robert said sullenly.

'He's lying,' Sara whispered. 'He likes to hurt people.'

'All right Sara!' There was exasperation in John's voice. 'You tell me, Robert. And forget that routine about "the woman tempted me." You're not Adam. And you can hardly expect me to believe that a hundred-and-fifteen-pound girl threw you around the room and made this mess!'

Robert shrugged his shoulders. He walked over to the desk, set the office chair back on its rollers, and sat down heavily. 'I came over to make a business deal,' he began. 'She offered to play house, so I——'

'He's lying,' Sara cried. 'He tried to rape me!'

'All right Sara!' John stomped over to the liquor cabinet without looking back at her, and poured himself a generous dollop of whiskey. He tossed it back with a single swallow, then slammed the glass back down on the shelf.

'Maybe I'd better tell *you* a story,' said John. He pulled the wingback chair to its feet and sank into it. 'I had a terrible night myself, Robert. I and two agents of the F.B.I. were at the plant tonight. We'd planned a little surprise, but our scam was interrupted by a bunch of outsiders who broke up the whole arrangement. Did you think you could get away with it for ever?'

His brother threw him a startled look. 'You knew?'

'Of course I knew. Anyone with half an eye could see what was happening. I figured your little game out two years ago!'

'But you let it continue?'

'What did you expect? You're my brother, damn it, not some strange bum from off the streets. I figured that sooner or later you'd get square with the world and settle down. But you didn't, did you? You just kept on digging yourself in deeper and deeper. I would have thrown you to the wolves a long time ago, but I did promise Mom!'

'So why are you doing it now? Why call in the F.B.I. now?'

'Good lord, Robert,' John sighed, 'you'll never understand me, will you? You're my brother. You could have had anything you asked for from me—you know that! If you'd wanted the farm, the factory, anything—all you had to do was ask!'

'Okay, so I'll ask!' There was a sarcastic look on Robert's face as he straightened up at the desk. He tightened his tie and sneered at his brother, 'For starters, I want Sara!'

'No, damn you! No!'

'See how quickly the tune changes,' Robert laughed. 'But why should I have to ask? How come you're the fair-haired boy? How come you got the farm, the money, the plant? Why should I have to ask? I'm a son of the family too! But no—everything for John, nothing for Robert! Well, to hell with you, John. I don't know anyone in this world I hate worse than I do you. Dear goody John, who can do no wrong. Don't worry, neighbours, for our John will make it all good and right! Well, I'm tried of begging. I'm tired of getting a few crumbs from your table. I'm *somebody* in this town, and I mean to be even bigger!'

'No, I'm afraid not,' John said coldly. 'You've had your chance, and then some. You know damn well why Dad left everything to me. You never did a day's work in your life! But when you went off to Harvard we all thought you'd turned the corner. Both Mom and Dad thought—well, I will say you made their last days happy.'

'Did that rankle with you, John? That I went to Harvard and made Phi Beta Kappa? Is that why you called in the F.B.I.? Can it be that big beautiful John is jealous of his little brother?'

John shook his head wearily. 'I didn't call the F.B.I.,' he said, 'they called me! I didn't mind the thought that half the country was being plastered with stolen Englewood I.C.s. But when the F.B.I. came to me with the report that all the guidance systems of the new Hungarian surface-to-surface missile were based entirely on the Englewood 53D electronic chip, that's where tolerance failed. Peddling on the black market is bad enough; peddling behind the Iron Curtain for offensive missile systems is just too much!'

He slammed his big fist down on the arm of the chair. The noise startled Sara. She had been sitting in a quiet daze, clinging to Mary's collar while the venom of the argument washed over her head. Her cheek was aching, her left wrist so painful that she dared not use it. The blood was still trickling down between her breasts from the gouge that Robert's ring had made.

'Those other men,' she said softly, 'I sent them. They were all volunteers from the union.'

He turned and stared at her. She ducked her head, and swung her hair out in front of her as a shield and a cover.

'*You* sent them? You? My God, just how many of our family troubles are you mixed up in? You are without a doubt the busiest busybody—are you all right, Sara?'

She waved off his interest with a flick of her hand. Her voice was too unsteady, too uncontrolled, for further use. She ducked lower into the shelter of Mary's body, commanding her nerves to stop transmitting those pulses of pain. John studied her for a moment, then turned his attention back to Robert.

'Now there's justice for you,' he said. 'Blind impartial justice. We'd planned a stake-out. We wanted to follow the truck to the delivery point, and keep things quiet, but it's too late now. The little girl you were beating up, sent her own task force. One of the men was wounded. The F.B.I. has infra-red movies of the whole thing. I expect that by morning they'll have their finger on the entire operation. And on you! There won't be much weaselling out from under this indictment!'

Anxiety spasms broke up Robert's face. There was a pleading look in his eye. 'But you *are* going to help me, aren't you? You're not going to stand there and watch me go down the tube! I *am* your brother!'

'It's a little late for you to remember that, isn't it? I haven't decided yet. But one thing is for sure—you're finished in this part of the world. Finished!'

They sat there, staring at each other. Each was angrily flushed, eyes gleaming.

'Elena!' Sara prompted. 'Ask him about Elena!'

'What?' John swung around towards her. 'What about Elena?'

Robert laughed, a high hysterical laugh that trembled at the point of breakage. 'Poor John,' he said. 'Hooked on two women in a row, and both of them whores!'

'Shut up!' his brother snarled at him. 'At least Sara is honest about it! What are you trying to tell me? That you've had Elena? You and half the county?'

'Yes!' Robert crowed. 'Plenty of times. And every time I laid her I laughed at you!'

'Is that why? Because she belonged to me? Is that why you were so eager to get Sara? Because she belongs to me too?'

'No! No, I——' Sara stammered. They paid her no attention.

'Yes!' Robert cried. 'Only this time I was going to get there first! How would you like that, brother?'

'You really are a bastard, aren't you! And all the time I thought it was something you'd grow out of! Now that we've got that far, *brother*, suppose you tell me where you were the night Elena fell down the stairs?' John rose from his chair and leaned over the desk, a dark vengeful figure of a man. His brother, although bigger than he, backed away from the confrontation, sliding his chair backward on its rollers. All the laughter had gone from his face. John leaned over farther and grabbed him by necktie and collar. He dragged Robert, chair and all, around the desk. Mary growled at them both. Slowly, gradually, John pulled Robert up from his chair, until they were standing toe to toe.

'Tell me the part I don't know,' he threatened in a

steel-cold voice. 'Were you here in this house when Elena died?'

'I—I—Yes, I was here,' Robert stammered. 'It wasn't a big thing! We were going to Florida for a week in the sun—that's all it was. I wasn't taking anything she didn't offer. You know that!'

'I know that—I've known it for years. She went to bed with any man she met as long as they were over eighteen and under eighty. Tell me what happened!'

'You're choking me. For God's sakes let me breathe!'

'I don't know why I should, damn you. Talk!'

'I got here late. She was already packed, and mad as a wet hen because I was late. She yelled at me about being chicken. She was already high as a kite. I was standing down here in the hall and she was upstairs on the landing. The kid was grabbing at her to keep her from going. He was screaming, she was screaming, and I was just about to leave. And then she started downstairs. She knocked the kid down to the floor, but just as she started down the stairs he managed to crawl after her and caught her shoe—and that was it. She came down the stairs head over heels and hit the floor with a terrible crack. Hell, there was no use even to look—I could hear her neck crack!'

John's grip tightened on his shirt front. 'But you didn't stop to check, did you?'

'I—No, I didn't. You know I can't stand that kind of thing. Blood and death, they bother me. As soon as I heard that crack I ran!'

'That's not the way I read it! You didn't run away immediately, *brother*. Tell me, why is Jackie so afraid of you? Tell me why he won't talk about that night?' John's hand twisted the collar tighter. Robert spluttered and gagged, and his knees buckled. John pulled him back up and relaxed his hold.

'All right,' Robert muttered. 'So I did. I dragged the damn kid down stairs and told him——'

'And told him what?'

'I told him the same thing could happen to him if he ever talked about it with anyone!'

'And if that doesn't send you straight to hell!' John roared. He pulled his brother by brute force out into the middle of the room. Sara ducked back against the corner of the sofa, hugging Mary against her. The dog was agitated, growling, and eager to get into the fight.

'You sentenced that kid to two years of torment,' John yelled. 'Two years in hell just because of you!' He dropped his grip on Robert's collar, and the two huge men stood tense for a moment. Then, without the slightest attempt on the part of either of them to defend themselves, they started to hammer away at each other in cold deliberation, as if each was trying to pound the other out of existence.

'No! No!' Sara screamed. They paid her no attention. She struggled to her feet, aching in every bone and muscle. 'No!' she screamed again. 'Stop it! You'll kill each other! Stop!' They made no sound save for heavy grunts as blows struck home in rhythmic destruction. Mary began to lunge towards the contestants. Sara struggled to maintain a grip on her collar, but was being dragged relentlessly towards the centre of the wild mêlée.

'John! You'll be hurt! Oh God, help me!' she screamed. She released Mary's collar, and both she and the dog threw themselves into the tiny area between the two men. She never knew whose hand it was that smashed against the side of her head just in front of her ear. She dropped to the floor between them like a poleaxed steer. Mary stood over the body, stiff-legged, and snapped at both men in turn, driving them back, and ending the fight.

When Sara fumbled her way back to consciousness it was morning. A beclouded sun was chasing filigrees of light across her bed, and the worried face of Mrs Emory was staring at her from a rocking chair beside the bed.

'Ah, you're back,' Mrs Emory said quietly. 'Can you move anything?'

Sara tried an experimental wiggle of her left foot, but the instant the muscles responded a lightning flash of pain crashed up into her brain. She moaned.

'Ah, there, lass,' the housekeeper soothed. 'Dr Fineberg has been and gone. He says you have multiple bruises, a sprained wrist, and a mild concussion. Don't try to talk too much.'

Sara tried three times to get the words to come out, and at last succeeded. 'John?' she pleaded.

'There now, John's fine. He sat with you most of the night, but then he had to go off someplace.'

'He's all right?'

'Who, John? He's fine—I told you. Was he at the same fight as you? Wow, what a mess in the living room! But the doctor said as soon as you wake up you were to take two of these pills.' One of her arms prodded Sara into sitting up. She gulped the two pills and washed them down with a splash of water. Every movement gave her pain. The housekeeper helped her back down, and waves of grey clouds enveloped her, burying her in their forgetfulness.

The next time she woke up it was late afternoon. Her head ached abominably, but she had to move. Her struggle to command her muscles brought a comforting hand to her aid.

'Bathroom,' she muttered, and felt herself swept up in strong arms. She struggled to open one eye. John's ear was bobbing in front of her. For some strange reason her other eye would not open. She was still in a daze, feeling no pain except for the headache. He kicked open the bathroom door and carried her in. Half an hour later she was settled in the easy chair by the window, packed in with pillows, her feet resting on an embroidery-covered footstool. There was still no pain, but her mind was hazy, and her vision indistinct.

'My eye?' she whispered.

John came closer to her, distorting as he did so. 'It's

only a bruise,' he said softly. 'I hit you—God, I feel like Adolf Hitler! I didn't mean to, believe me. I love you.'

'I know,' she returned. 'I've always known.'

'Sara,' he continued, 'I didn't realise. Until I brought you up to bed and undressed you, I didn't realise what he'd done to you.'

'I'll be all right,' she sighed, and faded away into darkness again.

The next time she awoke it was morning again, and Jackie was sitting by her bed. She felt much better. Her arms and legs seemed to function, although her left wrist was sore, and her cheek felt very tender.

'Hi, guy,' she called to him. He raced over from the window seat where he had been lounging. 'How come you're not in school?'

'I couldn't go without you,' he replied. 'Daddy's gone to Boston, and Mrs Emory is too busy, and Uncle Frank has an emergency with the gypsy moths, and so I——'

'What you're saying is that you decided to skip school?'

'I couldn't go and leave you alone like this, could I?' demanded Jackie.

'Where's Mary?' asked Sara. 'She usually looks after me very well.'

'Mary's not feeling very well. Uncle Frank took her to the vet's last night. She hurt her shoulder, and they gave her a shot or something. She's sleeping beside my bed.'

'Beside *your* bed? Are you making a pet out of my guard dog?'

'I—you know what, Sara?'

'What?'

'I think I better go to school,' he said hastily. 'G'bye.'

'No, you don't, you little monster. You'll either give me back my dog or give me a kiss before you go!'

'And that's another thing!' declared Jackie.

'Another what thing?'

'All that kissing and stuff.'

'Well, my dog or my kiss. Which?'

'Darn it!' he retorted. But he bent over the side of the bed and kissed her full on the lips, his skinny arms circling her neck as he did so. Sara lay back in the bed and smiled as she heard him clatter down the stairs.

The day stretched long before her. Every two hours Mrs Emory popped into the room and administered two pills. Each time she did so Sara slipped back into her daze, her peaceful painless daze. A light soup, which she had to drink through a straw, satisfied her at noon. In the afternoon she managed to get up under her own steam, to tend to her needs. The full-length bathroom mirror glared back at her. Her eye was swollen shut, and bruises in black and blue and green could be seen through her thin nightgown. 'Holy terrors,' she teased herself, 'a Sara Anderson horror production, with colour by Englewood!'

She staggered back to the bedroom, and settled herself in a chair. It was then, just before sundown, that he came. He stuck his head around the door, saw her sitting up, and walked in quietly. There seemed to be something distant, something cold about his attitude. He walked over beside her chair and brooded over her. She could see some cuts and abrasions on his face, and furrows of tiredness.

She broke the silence. 'What's wrong, John?'

'I don't know,' he mumbled. 'I guess I'm just tired. This thing with Robert has taken a lot out of me. And then you.'

'And then me?'

'Why did you do it?' he queried.

'Do what?'

'My God, have you even forgotten it? The day before yesterday. I went downtown as happy as a clam, would you believe it? I went down to get us a marriage licence! And there you were, coming out of that hotbed motel with not one but two men. You surely meant it when you said you liked the older ones. For God's sakes, if you needed money I would have given you some. You didn't have to go back into the trade to make a buck!' There was anguish in his voice.

'I was so damn mad,' he continued, 'that I drove all the way to Boston and back before I cooled down. And the two traffic tickets I got for speeding didn't help a bit, either! But I'll tell you something——'

Whatever it was he had planned to tell her got lost in the shuffle. Jackie came running up the stairs and barged into the room. 'It's the F.B.I.!' he shouted to his father. 'Downstairs. It's the F.B.I., and they want you, Daddy!' Both of them hurried out of the door.

Sara staggered back to bed. She tried unsuccessfully to read, but was unable to focus her eyes. Supper included a complete liquid diet. It tasted like dishwater. He did not come back. When she fell into an unsettled sleep she was haunted by nightmares.

He did not come the next morning, either. Mrs Emory came in regularly, but could provide no news. In the afternoon Sara refused her medications. The pain was still there, but she feared her dreams more than the physical pain. She was able to move now, albeit with difficulty. She spent the afternoon in the easy chair, staring glumly out the window at the rain-splattered clouds. Her mind was running around in circles. And at the end—or the beginning—of each circle was John. She pictured him in all manners—in silhouette, in full face, in love—but that was the trouble. She seemed to float along the edges of light, hearing everything, seeing everything, understanding nothing.

'Why, I've solved all the problems,' she told herself. 'I've solved Jackie's problem. I've solved Robert's problem, and I've solved John's problem. But I haven't solved Sara's problem!' Startled, she sat up straight in the chair and groaned as her muscles complained. Sara's problem? The problem with Sara was Sara! Poor brash bold Sara, who always rushed in where angels—poor Sara. She had casually kissed a stranger on the beach, a man she didn't even like, and she had never recovered!

She felt driven, as she had never been driven before. And what did John feel? 'Well, at least she's an honest whore!' And he had not come back! What else did he have to say to her? Obviously nothing. He had finished the message, punctuated it with his absence. She groaned, unable to separate phantom from reality, totally confused. Over and over she recounted his words like the beads on her rosary, and always she came back to that last incantation, 'an honest whore!' And she knew finally that nothing could be built on such a foundation.

She shook her head, still unable to comprehend. Somehow she had come home to safe harbour, and found she could not get across the sandbar. Befuddled by pain, confused by the drugs she had taken, shocked by her emotions, she struggled to her feet. She managed to find and open her two suitcases, and stuffed her clothes into them, helter-skelter. Jackie must have been attracted by the noise. He came into her room, his eyes wide as silver dollars.

'Sara?' he called. 'Sara?' She waved him away, unable to say a word. He drew back into the bathroom and watched as she staggered between the bed, where the suitcases lay, and the wardrobe. She had cleared hardly half of her clothes when the effort began to tire her. Wearily she staggered back to the bed and snapped down the covers of the suitcases. When she tried to lift them off the bed she found that she did not have the strength. Shaking her head in confusion, she gave up the effort. She picked up her large nurse's shoulder-bag, dumped its contents on the floor, and stuffed it with some of her flimsies, a blouse, and a set of jeans. She swung it all up on her shoulder, and then checked her handbag.

She had only a few cents in change, but her credit cards were all present. As she started for the door she remembered that she had no shoes. She fumbled in the closet, found a pair of weatherbeaten sandals, and thrust her feet into them.

Still in a daze, totally confused, she clutched urgently at Mary's collar and wobbled towards the door.

'Sara? No, Sara!' the little boy screamed. He ducked by her and ran down the stairs, continuing to scream at the top of his lungs.

Sara turned away from the main staircase and walked down the hall, out of the family living area, to the back stairs. She felt her way down in the dark, and out the back door. The little VW Bug was still sitting where she had last parked it, and the keys were in her bag.

She urged Mary into the back seat, then managed to squeeze herself behind the wheel. Her muscles ached. So great was the physical pain that it blocked out her mental anguish. She moved mechanically, started the engine, manoeuvred the clutch, and drove down the gravel road in second gear. As she did, her eyes reported, but her brain did not record the fact that an uproar was going on in the house behind her, and that the lights in every room were being turned on, one after another.

She turned south on the River Road and wobbled slowly down the two-lane highway in the gathering dusk, unhampered by other traffic. She knew that she was unfit to travel, so when she came to the parking lot of the Avery Maple Sugar Company she pulled off the road, drove into the deepest part of the lot, and parked.

She locked all the doors, climbed into the back seat and, comforted by the warmth of Mary's body, fell into a deep sleep. So she missed completely the sight of the heavy Chrysler that roared up and down the county road twice during the night, driven by a madman.

CHAPTER TEN

IT was almost six in the evening when Sara woke up in her own bed in the house on Point Judith. She had used all day Monday to cover the usual three-hour drive from Deerfield to the coast, and had fallen into the downstairs bed, too weak to make it up the stairs to the loft. She was still unable to reconcile herself to what had happened. And she was certainly not the Sara Anderson she had been. Not only her strength of muscle had failed her, but her strength of mind as well. There were black fears nestling in the recesses of her mind. Her mad encounter with Robert had pierced all her defences. In one hour he had wiped out her lifetime of experience with her brothers. She could no longer believe that all big men were gentle giants, willing captives. She had lost all her self-assurance, and needed someone to cling to.

When she struggled out of bed she hugged Mary as if the dog were her only life raft in a dark sea. The dog, feeling her tension, followed her every step, rubbing against her legs occasionally to give assurance. Every sharp noise caused Sara to jump. Even the raucous screech of the seagulls startled her.

Her battered body was too sensitive to bear heavy clothes. She had clumsily manoeuvred herself into a lightweight nightgown, struggled to make a cup of coffee, and fried two eggs. She sat at the kitchen table until the coffee was cold and the eggs congealed, without attempting a sip or a bite. At eight o'clock she clicked on one light, scraped her dish into the garbage pail, and got herself into the shower.

The pressure of the water was too much for her tender skin. Before she could get a quick rinse the pain forced her to shut off the water. As she struggled to step

167

out of the tub she heard the front door open and shut. Mary, who had been standing beside the tub while she showered, walked to the bathroom door and gave the 'Whuff' that signalled a close friend.

'Sara? Sara? Where you are? It is me, Maria Louisa.'

'In the shower,' Sara called weakly. 'Be out in a minute!'

The footsteps came across the living room and into the bathroom. 'Eh, Sara,' Maria said, 'Mamma sees the light of you house, no? She says Aha, Sara have come home and find nothing to eat, no? So to bring the soup, Maria! I put it on the table of you, and—*Madre de Dios*! What have happen to you back and all over?'

'It's nothing,' Sara reassured her. 'I fell down some steps, that's all.'

The little Puerto Rican girl walked around Sara, who was vainly trying to cover herself with a small hand towel. 'Is a funny thing,' she commented. 'When you fall all down those stairs you get fingerprints on you shoulders, no? I gonna tell Papa!' And before Sara could argue the point, Maria was gone.

Sara dried herself carefully, patting rather than rubbing. She slipped her nightgown back on, snapped out the light, and sat in the darkness, looking out at the cold grey sea. Cold and grey. My whole life looks like that, she told herself bitterly. She took two pills and staggered back to bed. Sleep came, but so did the nightmares. She tossed and screamed until she woke herself up, and then was too fearful to go back to sleep again. When the morning brought a north-easter, and gale winds whipped the Sound, rattling the cottage windows, it matched her mood.

For the next two days she sat huddled in a corner, clutching Mary close to her for comfort. Neighbours came each day with food, but she could not eat. She was unable to make her mind a blank. Everything she thought, everything she saw, was conditioned by her memories of John. One half of her mind and all of her body screamed that she loved him. The other half of her mind remembered all those cold hateful words, and that look of anguish, of loathing. Love and hate! Caught between two opposing emotions of equal power, she bounced around in her mind like a skiff caught in a riptide. But she did not cry. She had no more tears to give.

When the storm finally blew out late on Wednesday night, she hobbled to the kitchen, heated a can of soup, and drank it off. Her stomach rebelled at the first food it had seen in three days, she managed to hold it down. There were lights in the big house on top of the hill behind her cottage, but she assigned no importance to them. She stumbled back to bed and stretched herself out, one hand over the edge of the bed, tangled in Mary's collar. The nightmares began again about midnight. In the shadows of her drugged and dazed mind she could hear someone screaming. It sounded far away, from some other girl, from some other time.

And then there was a loud noise, a crash, and suddenly she felt herself surrounded in warmth, in love, protected. The screaming stopped. She nestled herself into this shelter, and faded into a natural sleep, comforted by the strong arms that encircled her.

It was not morning light that awakened her, but rather the uneasy stirring of the shoulder on which her head lay. She blinked her eye open and admired the tendrils of wavy black hair that tickled her nose. It took a moment to register that she was sharing her bed with a full grown male, fully clothed—one she knew very well. Her movements awakened him. He gently lifted her head and shifted it lower on to his chest.

'I think my arm is falling off,' he groaned. 'Is the service satisfactory, modom?'

'Why—what are you doing here?' she stammered.

'Waiting for you to wake up,' he said innocently. 'It's damnably hard to seduce a girl when she insists on sleeping through my best efforts.'

'Oh, you——' she spluttered. 'You ass! What are you doing here in my house in my bed when you should be in South Deerfield?'

'Well, we were sitting around the house—Jackie and I were—when we heard this woman screaming. So Jackie said to me, 'Why don't you go and see?' And we did. And it was you, sitting up straight in your bed in that peekaboo nightgown, yelling your head off. Hungry?'

'Why—I—Yes I am,' said Sara, too bemused to be able to follow the conversation. 'Only I have to run to the bathroom, and I can't run!'

'All services provided!' John folded her blankets back, slipped an arm under her knees, and swung her up off the bed.

'Stop it!' she yelled at him. Her eyes were sparking for the first time. 'This nightgown——'

'Is certainly made to be seen!' he laughed. 'Why, the gown is so beautiful that one could hardly notice the beautiful girl inside it. You are inside it, aren't you?'

'John—don't tease. I really don't feel too strong!'

He was immediately penitent, resting her on the edge of the bed while he gently wrapped her in a robe. His arm supported her as she made her way next door to the bathroom, and then he escorted her to a comfortable chair at the table.

'I can walk much better,' she announced as she collapsed in the chair.

'That's good,' he remarked. 'You and I have a lot to talk about, young lady, but first I have to take Mary for a run. That shoulder of hers is still bothering her. I've made breakfast, and Jackie will serve it.'

Sara watched as he walked out the door. Mary followed him without question. 'Almost as if he were already in possession!' she muttered under her breath. The thought was breathtaking!

'What?' Jackie asked as he came in from the kitchen, arms loaded.

'Nothing,' she replied. 'I was talking to myself.'

'Here's breakfast. Dad made it. It ain't nothin' like what Mrs Gregory makes.'

She looked down at her plate, where two pieces of

overdone toast crowded against each other as if to bolster their loneliness. 'You made this?' she asked.

'Not me!' Jackie stoutly defended himself. 'Dad. Mrs Emory says he needs a keeper.'

'Your father is a very remarkable man,' she lectured him. 'We mustn't expect him to do *everything* in the world. What else did Mrs Emory say?'

'She told Dad I needed a full-time mother, and he'd better not blow this one cause if he came home without one this time she was gonna quit.'

'Oh my! This—er—toast is very—toasty. You want a nibble?'

'Nope—it's burnt. I had my breakfast. Me and Dad ate already. I hope you feel better by lunch time, Sara!'

'What did your dad make you for breakfast?' she asked.

'Peanut butter sandwiches, and a glass of milk.'

'Ah. Very nutritious,' she said cautiously. 'Yes. I suspect I'll be better by noontime—or we'll all starve!'

'You want your coffee now?'

'Oh! There's more? Yes, I'm ready for my coffee. Can you carry it by yourself?'

'Of course! What did you think anyway?'

'Yes, I'd forgotten. Bring it out and I'll give it a try. Your dad made this too? This instant coffee?'

'Yes,' Jackie replied as he sat the mug down before her. 'It don't look right. At least not like Mrs Emory makes it!' He sat down at the table beside her and watched as she sipped. 'Good?'

She made a face. 'Not exactly, dear,' she reported. 'It seems to have a little too much flavour. How much coffee did your dad put in the cup?'

'Two tablespoons.'

'You sure? You mean those big spoons?'

'Yeah. Taste good?'

'Well, I would rather not answer that. How come you're not in school?'

'Dad said it wasn't no use. He said we had to settle your hash first, and then we'd see about school. What does that mean, settle your hash?'

'I—I'm not quite sure. I suppose he means about my job and so on. You expect to be here long?'

'He said—my dad said—does it get very cold around here?'

'Only in the late winter. January, February, like that.'

'I guess we'll be here until then, at least. My dad, he said we was gonna stay here until Hell freezes over. Is that likely to be very long?'

'Oh? That sounds like a pretty long time. What else did your dad say?' asked Sara.

'His dad said stop pumping the kid!' The door had banged open, admitting a blast of fresh air, a dog, and John. 'Mary's movement isn't too bad,' he told her. 'She can run a little. But I think that tomorrow we'd better take her to the vet's. Jackie, why don't you take Mary for a long slow walk up the beach? I need to talk to Sara.'

'But he doesn't know the area. He might get lost!'

'What you mean is that you don't want to be alone with me, girl. What's the matter now? Scared?'

'Yes, she confessed ruefully, but by this time Jackie and Mary had already disappeared through the door.

'And just to make sure——' said John, and walked over and threw the bolt on the door. 'Now, little girl, you've led me one hell of a chase!'

'Oh?' she asked, looking for a diversionary subject. 'How's Robert?'

'To hell with Robert,' he growled. He pulled up a chair and sat beside her, pulling her own chair out from the table to face him. 'Robert's fine. You really know how to break up a fight! I offered him enough money to go to Honduras, but he decided he'd stay and face the music. He's going to testify for the Government. The F.B.I. has him stored away in a safe house someplace— I don't know where. I'm glad of it; he's the only brother I've got. Now, let's talk about you and all the lies you told me.'

'Lies? I've never told you a lie in my whole life!' Her

eyes sparkled with anger. For a moment the old Sara had returned.

'So half the truth is still a lie, little girl. Ralph told me all about you!'

'Ralph told you? You've seen Ralph?'

'Yes, I've seen Ralph. And I've talked to David. You remember him? The gangster down in Dallas who plays for the Dallas Cowboys. I don't know how I missed that one. He's on the sports pages every week. And I talked to Jim—you remember, the guy in the drug business?'

'Well, he is. They are. It's all true!' Sara ducked her head, trying to hide behind the fall of her hair. John cupped her chin and forced her to look up at him.

'The first thing you have to learn, little girl, is that we're going to be a team. And in any team only one can be the boss—and that's me.'

'We are? You—you are?'

'Shut up!' he ordered. 'First things first. I told you about seeing you come out of that damn motel with those two men. But then I got interrupted by the F.B.I.'

'You said—you made a terrible remark. And then you said you got so mad you raced off to Boston. And I'm not! I'm not, and I told you so before!'

'I know you're not. Shut up!'

'You know——' Sara began.

'I said shut up. And come over here.' John picked her up and swung her to his knees, cuddling her head against his chest. 'Now—I told you what I saw, and what I thought. But before I rushed off to Boston I *still* went down to the Town Hall and got a marriage licence!'

'Even when you thought I was a—I can't even say that word!'

'Even when. Shut up. Don't you ever do what you're told?'

She snuggled up against him, and he continued the story. 'So I had an appointment with the F.B.I. already. You knew about that. And then that crazy fight. And then I had a stroke of genius. I figured that what really was disturbing you was that Pudge wasn't with you. Any woman would want her own baby with her, especially when she was about to——'

'You really mean it? You wanted me and Pudge too?'

'How many times do I have to tell you to shut up? Certainly. You and Pudge and the dog and half of Bristol County, if that's what it took to get you. Where was I?' John reached out idly and picked up her coffee cup. 'Oh yeah. So I figured what you'd told me. Ralph was in the numbers racket in Boston—and he had a kid. I didn't even know his last name. Dear God, what is this swill?' He had stopped to take a sip of coffee, and was vainly looking for some place to spit it out.

'It's coffee, I'm given to understand,' Sara said very primly. 'You don't like it?'

He slammed the cup down on the table. 'Woman, you're going to get yours one of these days!' he threatened.

'I hope so,' she whispered under her breath. 'I certainly hope so!'

'What?' he asked. He managed to squeeze a handkerchief out of his pocket and wiped his mouth. 'Where was I. Oh yeah. I drove down to Boston— I have a couple of friends on the police force—and for two days they and I tried to find Ralph in the numbers business. No luck. All because of you. And then on the third day I was driving out of the parking lot of the Marriot, and there was this big billboard. I'd seen it every day, but never looked at it. 'Have you Tried Your Number Today?' it said. And then down in the corner, 'Ralph P. Anderson, Chairman, Massachusetts State Lottery Commission!' In the numbers business! I should wash your mouth out with soap! So I went to see him. I was prepared to punch him in the mouth and steal the kid, you know. Why the devil didn't you tell me he was so big?'

'Who, Ralph? He's not big. He's the smallest of all the boys. Wait till you see David. He should have been named Goliath!'

'Well, anyway, I've talked to them all. And I had supper with Sylvia and Pudge. And now I know all about you, Susan Antonia. And what the devil are you crying about?'

'I don't know,' she sobbed. 'I don't know. I'm so happy! What are you going to do next?'

'This.' He leaned her back in his arms and gently brushed his lips across hers. Despite all her aches and pains the spark was still there. She threw her arms around his neck and clung to him until the pain of movement caused her to wince. John released her at once.

'Still hurts?' he probed. She nodded. 'What you need is to soak in a nice warm bath for a while,' he said. Before she could agree or disagree he stood up and carried her back to her bedroom. He laid her gently down on the bed, then went next door. She could hear the water running in the tub, and could see steam coming out of the bathroom door. She stretched out languorously on the bed. Her left eye opened slightly, a sure sign that the swelling was receding. John was back before she could do anything else.

'Now,' he ordered as he unbelted her robe, 'slip out of all this stuff.' He had her shoulders out of her nightgown before she could register a protest. 'But——' she stammered. He stopped up her mouth with his, but his hands continued to undress her.

'Here we go,' he announced, swinging her up in his arms again.

'But you can't carry me around without any clothes on!'

'Did you expect to take a bath in your nightgown? Your brother David told me how to handle you. Shut up!'

'Okay—I know,' she sighed. 'Shut up. What did David say?'

'Someday I'll tell you. Not now. Is the water too warm?'

She sank down into the luxurious warmth and

sighed. 'No. It's fine.' She tried to sink down out of sight in the water. 'But there's no soapsuds,' she protested feebly. No matter how low she squirmed the tips of her breasts were above water. But it made no difference; in the clear water he could see everything anyway! 'Are you going to just stand there and watch me?'

'Not me,' he laughed. He stripped off his sweater, leaving himself nude to the waist. He hummed a tune she couldn't remember as he reached for the washcloth, lathered it on the soap bar, and began to gently scrub off her toes and ankles. As he made the progression upwards she rioted in the combination of sensations. The warmth of the water, the movement of his hands, all tangled her mind. She lay back in the tub and gloried in it. Her movement splashed excess water down the overflow drain, and took twenty-four years of narrow inhibitions with it. She gloried in it all. Some minutes later she noticed that John had arrived at her breasts, generously laving them in the soft soap, and caressing her gently in a circular motion.

'John?' she called to him. He was too entranced by what he was doing. 'John?' she repeated, then tugged at a wayward curl that was tumbling over his eye.

'Hmm?' He came out of his trance and looked at her.

'I think you've lost the washcloth,' she suggested gently, 'and the water's getting cold.'

'Yes,' he retorted dreamily. 'When I went by your knees. They're very—bumpy. Does it bother you?'

'Yes, it does,' she chuckled, 'but we have to stop anyway!'

He smiled back at her, and helped her out to dry and dress.

'Dry your hair,' he ordered. 'There's a beautiful sun outside, and we ought to get some of it.' He made as if to go.

'Please,' she begged with her eyes as well as her voice, 'I don't want to be alone. I need you.'

'What is this?' he asked. 'What's happened to my bold brash Sara?'

'I don't know.' But of course she did know, and didn't dare to tell him.

She pushed her stiffened muscles to their limit, and concocted hot soup and toasted cheese sandwiches for lunch.

'Best meal I've had since we came,' Jackie commented, then ducked as his father swung an exaggerated fist at him.

'Professors of Engineering don't have to be able to cook?' Sara asked.

'No,' he replied. 'When they get hungry they marry a cook.'

'Oh?' she queried politely. But he shifted the conversation.

'Out in the sunshine,' he commanded. 'Everybody. Sara, you and I need to take a walk. Jackie, I noticed there's a barbecue pit by the side of the house. You go down on the beach and get some of that wood the storm threw up.'

'Driftwood,' she contributed. 'And you have to have a Town permit to build an open fire. Clean Air Law.'

'Yeah, driftwood,' he repeated. John was laughing down at her. It was a strange proprietorial laugh, she thought to herself. 'And I got one yesterday.' He helped her gently into her light plastic windbreaker.

'Out of the wind it's warm,' he advised. She started to plait her hair, but he put a stop to it by holding both her small hands in one of his. 'Let it blow,' he ordered. 'I like it that way.'

She looked up at him speculatively. The old Sara would have snapped at him and braided her hair the way she wanted it. This new Sara seemed to fumble around for words. 'Yes, sir,' she finally managed to choke out.

'And besides,' he told her, 'you've got a beaut of a black eye. The hair will help you hide it.'

She followed him out of the door into the sunshine.

The sky was a freshly-swept blue, the intense colour that a storm leaves behind it. She took a deep breath and looked up at him, the long, lean love of him. 'You've got a beaut yourself,' she said maliciously. 'Didn't duck, did you?'

'You should see the other guy,' he returned. 'Say, those *are* beautiful flowers you've got there. This whole peninsula is nothing but a sand dune. How did you get flowers to grow?'

'It's the soil,' she replied. 'Me and Ralph, we carried it down here in buckets from Grandpa Carter's farm.'

'Ralph and I,' he corrected her automatically.

'Yes. Him and me.'

'Your brother Ralph.'

'Yes, him.' As they walked down on to the beach she kicked at a pebble and sprayed a film of sand before them. But she had to know! 'What did Ralph tell you to——'

'Advised me,' he interrupted. 'He advised me.'

'Well,' she gulped, 'what did Ralph advise you to do?'

'He *advised* me to take a firm hand with you. He also suggested that I might beat you from time to time.'

'Ralph said that? He wouldn't *ever* say that!'

'Perhaps not exactly that way. What he said was that you were a spoiled brat in your youth, and that you hadn't improved too much. He also said that you had a heart of gold, and since nothing else seemed to work, perhaps a beating now and then might have some results.'

He looked down and smiled at her chagrin, and her blazing eyes. 'Don't take it to heart,' he chuckled. 'I'm glad to see my spitfire still spitting. Your brother Ralph is a city boy. Us country boys know that you gentle a filly to the halter with a firm hand and a lot of love!'

'And is that what you think you're doing, John Englewood?' she raged at him. 'You think you're breaking me to a halter?'

'That's my girl!' he laughed. 'But of course with a

filly it only works when she doesn't know what's coming next.'

'I don't want to talk to you any more,' she grumbled. 'You're just another big male chauvinist. I know all about you people. I grew up with three of you!'

They walked slowly up the beach. John was being careful, she noted, to match his strides to hers. She kept her head down, knowing that he was watching her. The wind whipped her hair into streamers. She was unable to contain a giggle, and her hand moved of its own volition and seized his. After a brief walk they turned back.

Harry Muldoon's dinghy was overturned in the sand above the highwater mark. They settled down in the lee of the craft, out of the wind. Not a word passed between them. Sara scaled a stone down into the water and watched as it skipped twice and dived under a whitecap. Out of the corner of her eye she could see John was doing the same. It was a big ocean, but he kept missing it. Oh well! she told herself.

Using both arms, she levered herself up and moved close beside him. His arm came around her and rested casually on her shoulder. She accepted the invitation, and snuggled close against him, drawing her legs up and resting her head on his chest. His other arm came around and supported her. 'Mmmm,' she murmured.

'Nice!' he replied. One of his hands wandered through the scattered mess of her hair, combing it out with his fingers. 'Silk,' he said. He nibbled at her earlobe in an alarming manner.

'I think I'll have to get it cut for the hot summer,' she offered, trying to evade being eaten alive.

'You do and I really *will* beat you,' he commented, and again that strange feeling of awareness ran up her spine. She decided that a manoeuvre was necessary. His invidious invasion of her senses had to be stopped somehow!

'What happened about the factory, and the board meeting?' she asked.

John knew a ploy when he heard one. He stopped nibbling, but with a sigh of regret. 'Robert gave me his proxy for all his shares,' he told her. 'So we met. We authorised an audit, then fired the management team, and elected a new president. By the way, we also voted another seat on the board for a union member. Mr Evans says he knows you, and sends his—what did he say—sincere admiration!'

'Yes, I know Skip. And you got to be elected President?'

'Who, me? Not on your life! I happen to have a very disagreeable Ph.D candidate at the University. A real organiser and doer. Heaven protect me from that type! He gets his degree in June. We elected him Vice-President for Operations. But then we got to talking, all of us, and it finally developed that the union wasn't prepared to halt the strike until we elected a President with a little heart—at least that's what Evans said. So we did. But only temporarily. I told them it could only be for a year—no longer.'

'Well, is it a big secret? Who?'

'You, that's who. Sara Anderson, President!'

'But I don't know anything about presidenting!' she protested. 'I'm a nurse. We have this lady downtown who gets calls, and we——'

'Don't give me that sarcastic tongue, woman. You're saying that maliciously. And I've already heard from Mrs Emory and Dr Fineberg the difference between call nurses and callgirls! Besides which, according to Evans, you're the only person in Pioneer Valley who seems to know anything about corporations!'

'But suppose I don't want to?' she asked diffidently. She was feeling apologetic. She *had* said it maliciously.

'I didn't plan to ask you,' he said firmly. 'It's done, a *fait accompli*. That's another thing Ralph advised. Well?'

'Yes,' she replied softly. And then after a moment's reflection, 'Yes, sir.'

John drew her closer, lifted her chin, and kissed her gently. 'You're learning, my dear,' he chuckled. 'Go slow and easy. It's not so bad. Everybody needs somebody.'

Which seemed to be as good a summary as anything, Sara thought as she got ready for bed that night. Both John and Jackie were sleeping upstairs in the loft 'in case you need us,' Jackie had explained. She scrubbed her teeth, braided her hair, and pulled out her sexiest see-through nightgown. 'A girl never knows when she might wake up screaming,' she told herself. 'It always pays to look one's best!' But when she woke up from a deep and untroubled sleep the sun was already high in the morning sky. She managed a robe over her nightgown, and felt a pang of regret that nothing had happened.

Jackie came rattling into the house as she prepared breakfast in the kitchen.

'Mary's not with you?' she asked as she poured him a glass of orange juice.

'Nope. Dad got up early and took her over to the vet's. He said to tell you he'd be back at noon. Is that ham and eggs?'

'Yes. Would you rather have sausages?'

'Nope. Too bad you won't have a chance to practise much. You're a good cook, Sara.' He gulped down the food as if manners had been outlawed by Constitutional law. Sara sipped at her coffee and wondered if she dared eat a big meal herself.

'What do you mean, I won't have a chance to practise?' she asked idly.

'Well, Dad said—Dad said keep my big mouth shut! And by the way, I have to break my contract with you. Business is business, you know.'

'Oh? Not satisfied with the service? I thought that I was pretty fair at this Rent-a-Mom business.'

'The service was fine,' Jackie assured her hurriedly. 'Just fine. But the price—well, you know how it is. I'm trying to set up a merger with a larger company.'

'I see,' she said, really not seeing at all. 'Want some more eggs?' He did, and in the bustle that followed, the original conversation got lost.

Cleaning. Sara's mind yelled at her as she looked around. Jackie had gone up the hill to the big house. Cleaning. The cottage looked like the original Briar Patch. So she changed into an old pair of jeans, and a faded blouse, and had at it—slowly. By noon her back ached. She stepped out into the warmth of the sun and rested for an hour on the veranda steps. At one o'clock Jackie came back for a moment.

'There's a family up there.' He waved excitedly in the direction of the Gomez cottage. 'The lady invited me to lunch. They have hamsters. Can I?' She waved approval and sat down again. It was two o'clock before she heard the car pull up in back of the house, and John and Mary came around the corner.

She hugged the great dog, and looked her over for damage. 'Nothing really wrong,' John reported. 'Just a bruised shoulder. They gave her a cortisone shot, and told her to take it easy.'

Sara had been too worried about Mary to look at him. Now, reassured, she did. 'Good heavens,' she cried, startled, 'your lip is bleeding! What happened?'

He smiled wryly. 'I had a conversation with your friends and neighbours,' he reported. 'I stopped by the general store up by the crossroads. There was a family up there—all men. They asked me to step outside with them.'

'It must have been the Brasher boys. They hit you?' Her voice showed her concern. She was almost in tears as she got up and dabbed rather ineffectively at his lip with her handkerchief.

'No, they didn't. They did make me an offer I could hardly refuse, though. They told me that the water here is very bad for people from the Deerfield area, and suggested that by Monday I ought to go back to Deerfield. How about that?'

'But they didn't hit you?'

'No. But they sure gave me cause to think. I've got to change all my plans! Tough neighbours you have here, girl.'

'Well, they're only trying to protect me, you know,' she explained. 'They all know I'm alone. They think I'm their baby sister, that's all. Who hit you?'

'I walked out of the store and there was this little guy—a dark thin face, moustache. Stood about five foot six, and maybe twenty yards wide.'

'Hernandes—Juan Hernandes. He's a Puerto Rican fisherman. He has three daughters of his own.'

'Yeah, well anyway, I started to walk by him, and he said something very uncomplimentary in Spanish. And then he reached back and clobbered me one time, and decked me!'

'With just one blow?' queried Sara.

'Yeah. Now, I figure that if that's what the little guys around here can do, I wouldn't want to tangle with the big boys!'

'Oh, John,' she sighed, 'it's really all my fault. As they see it, you took me away, so you were responsible for me. And then Maria Luisa saw me in the shower, and——'

'And the truth is that they're right, and I should have protected you, and I didn't. Stop worrying your head, girl. I'm going to do something about it—I'd better, or I'll get my head handed to me! Come on, we have some shopping to do.'

'But Jackie is away.'

'I just saw Jackie. He's fine. Mary can watch him. Come on.'

What am I doing? Sara asked herself as she followed him around the house. Him master, me slave? Why don't I say something? Why don't I be smart and witty? Why don't I floor him with some short pithy comment? Why don't I——

'Get in the car,' ordered John.

'Yes,' she responded. 'Yes, sir!'

He looked so competent sitting behind the wheel.

Every movement was a measure of grace. He treats his car like a fond living thing. He treats everything he owns with love, she told herself, and a shiver ran down her spine. Hoping he would not notice, she moved a little closer and put her hand on his knee. He noticed. He turned briefly from the road and smiled at her. I wonder if he would like to own a harem slave? Sara asked herself.

He drove them into the town of Marion, an old New England town, sprinkled with large white houses, two brick churches, and a town square dedicated to the men of the War of 1812. They turned right on South Main Street, and stopped before a little boutique with a sign outside that said 'Louise.'

John took her hand and led her into the shop. It was dark inside, out of the sun. He could see the salesgirl run her practised eye up and down Sara's form. Note. Worn denims, with a tear at the knee. Battered faded blouse. Pigtails. What a blackeye. Pigtails, would you believe it? And the man? Tall, nice-looking in an ugly sort of way. Black pullover, jeans. Canvas sneakers!

'My little girl needs a dress,' said John, sinking down into one of the fragile chairs. 'A wedding dress. Something lacy and demure.'

'I do?' Sara squeaked.

'And we have to take it with us. She's size——'

'Eight, I would suppose,' the salesgirl said.

'Yes. A perfect size eight.'

'I am not!' She struggled to get into the conversation. 'Nobody's perfect. I'm—well, perhaps you didn't notice, but I'm somewhat—topheavy. I need a size ten.'

'Yeah,' he chuckled, 'I noticed. I noticed. A perfect size ten.'

'We're a little expensive here,' the salesgirl said doubtfully. 'And if you want it right away it would cost considerably more. Perhaps you'd do better at the Mall?'

'Perhaps,' said John, pulling a roll of fifty-dollar bills out of his pocket. 'Shall we get on with it?' The salesgirl bustled out.

Sara found herself standing in front of him like an embarrassed schoolgirl. She clasped both hands behind her back to restrain herself from pummelling him, and kicked at a fold in the rug. When she had mastered her moment of rage she glared at him. 'Am I thinking of getting married?' she asked.

'Yes,' he replied. 'I think I'll smoke this cigar while we wait.'

'I don't like——' and she stopped to consider. 'Am I thinking of getting married very soon?' she asked.

'Very soon,' he agreed.

Sara found it difficult to think. For some reason all her logic had taken flight. John was being a dictatorial insufferable male, and yet the bait in his trap was so attractive. She wondered if she dared another question. He picked up a copy of *Cosmopolitan* and began to study the pictures. Which seemed to answer her doubts.

'Thank you,' she muttered.

The rest of the day was anti-climax. It took two hours for the hastily summoned seamstress to take in and let out. And then the matching accessories took another hour. John criticised everything, made all the selections, and left her with nothing to say and no time to say it. On the way home she asked soberly, 'I suppose I may chose my own underwear?'

'Sarcasm?' he asked.

'Oh no. No!' she hastened to assure him. And since that was all the information she could get out of him, she plastered on a smile of indifference, made supper, and finally went to bed, with her questions still unanswered. 'What's come over you, Sara Anderson?' she demanded after she slipped under the sheets. 'That man wants cutting down to size! What I ought to do is rise up in Biblical wrath and smite him hip and thigh!' The idea had a certain attraction, and she was blushing as she fell into a deep sleep.

Saturday passed as a hurricane passes. Everybody else bustled and ran errands, and held secret conferences, while Sara sat passively in the eye of it all, trying to find

out what was going on. Even Mary was suspect. She
called the dog over to her chair, and Mary came and
rested her jaw in Sara's lap. 'You know, don't you!'
Sara demanded. The big eyes blinked at her, and the
bigger tongue came out and licked Sara's nose. 'Damn!'
Sara moaned, eaten up by curiosity. 'Who *can* you trust!'

But Sunday was different. After an early breakfast,
John and Jackie hurried up the hill to the big house,
and returned shortly dressed in tie and jacket. 'Church!'
he told her. Sara shrugged her shoulders, found a
proper dress, and climbed into it. In respect to the
essentially Latin congregation, she pinned a tiny lace
mantilla into her coronet, slipped into a pair of
broidered flats, and joined them.

They walked to the church through sparkling
sunlight. A cool small breeze flirted with the hem of her
skirt. Jackie clung to her right hand, and her left rested
in the crook of John's arm. Me and my family, she
thought, and felt a burst of pride.

Most of the congregation was waiting in the small
parking lot outside the church. There was something
cautiously strange about the way they were greeted. No
words were exchanged. The crowd seemed to open in
front of them, then close behind them, without a sound.
Sara led her two men down to her regular pew, blessed
herself, then settled back into the comfortable tradition
of the Mass. John aped her movements, but did not go
forward to the altar to partake. When the service was
over, Father Flanagan went from the altar to the pulpit,
a variation from routine which stilled the buzzing in the
church.

'My dear people,' Father Flanagan announced, 'with
the approval of our Bishop, I am authorised to
announce that tomorrow morning at ten o'clock it
shall be my pleasure to unite in marriage Susan
Antonia Rebecca Anderson, spinster of this Parish,
with Mr John Francis Englewood, of—er—Deerfield,
Massachusetts.' The good Father's lips pursed, as if
some of the words tasted badly.

The entire congregation stood, and remained in the pews while Sara and John and Jackie made their way out of the church. He put his arm around her waist and hugged her gently as they walked out. As they passed each pew the people standing there followed. Out into the bright sunlight they went, like two Pied Pipers pulling a long chain of followers behind them.

'Right here on the grass,' said John. He pulled her to a stop. 'Isn't it strange? Just like the first day we met. Remember?'

'I remember everything about you,' she confessed. 'Right here what?'

'Don't you remember how you got Mary to stop biting me?'

'Yes?' Her voice was hesitant.

'Well, come on, kiss me! Do I have to do everything for myself?'

'Aha!' she she exclaimed. 'So that's the plan. I kiss you in public and the population stops trying to beat your brains out! Suppose I refuse?'

'You wouldn't dare,' he sighed. 'Come on, hurry up.'

'A girl likes to be asked,' Sara suggested coldly.

'You don't want to get married tomorrow?'

'Yes, of course I do, but——'

'Now you've been asked. Kiss me!'

So she hurried, stretching up on tiptoe to reach around his neck and bring his head down. His lips sealed hers in a long satisfying promise that made her spine tingle. As she struggled back to the present she could hear a round of applause from the congregation. John released her, took her arm, and led her homeward. Jackie and Mary had disappeared.

'I arranged for them to spend the day with the Gomez family,' he explained. When they reached the house, they sat in the sunshine on the veranda. John struggled out of his coat and tie, then leaned over and took her shoes off. She was puzzled, but wiggled her toes in relief.

'So I didn't have to wait for David to come and blow

my house down,' he laughed. 'You've done that all by yourself!'

It gave Sara a great sense of satisfaction to agree with him entirely, but in her new caution she ducked her head and said, 'If you say so, darling.'

'Your Father Flanagan gave me a hard time, you know.'

'Oh dear. About the banns?'

'No. About the spelling.'

'Spelling? Englewood isn't hard to spell.'

'No, but he had a difficult time with Congregationalist! By the way, David can't come—they have a pre-season game. Jim and his wife will be in tonight. Frank and Mrs Emory will meet them at the airport and bring them down. Ralph will be here tomorrow morning. Sylvia will stand up for you. David sent extreme regrets. He said he might break a finger and come anyway!'

'But——' Sara decided to take the bull by the horns. 'What was the—the advice that David gave you?'

'About the same as Ralph. He said you were terribly spoiled, and the only way for me to keep control was to keep you barefoot and pregnant!' As if to emphasise the point, he reached down and put her shoes in his pocket.

'Oh!' she gasped. 'That man——'

'Sounded very sensible to me,' John said calmly. 'In fact, that's why I told them at the Plant you could only be President for a year. Your wheeling and dealing days are over, Sara Anderson!'

'How—how many children are you planning to have?'

'Are *we* planning to have—*we*! About three. That's a nice number, spaced two years apart. Have I forgotten anything?'

'Well, really!' she announced, ducking her head to hide the gleam in her eye. 'You men are all the same! You can have your fun in an hour, but I have to work nine months at each one! There's a great deal of time involved, and I can't afford to waste a minute getting started!'

'Yes. Well, after the wedding and the reception tomorrow——'

'I'll be very tired. I might even have a headache. I'm sure I'll have a headache. But I feel fine right now!'

'My mother told me about girls like you,' he laughed.

She nuzzled closer to him, catching up his hand in both of hers, and pressing it against the softness of her breast. 'Yes?' she asked innocently. 'What did she tell you?'

'She told me that when I found one, I should hold her and cherish her, and never miss a moment,' John chuckled. He stood up, towering over her, then reached down and whipped her into his arms. Sara pressed her lips against the tender spot of his throat, where his pulse was racing in a mad gallop, and giggled as he carried her over the threshold.

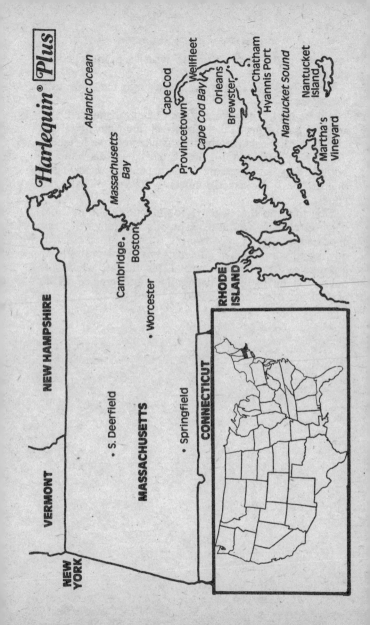

Great old favorites...
Harlequin Classic Library

The **HARLEQUIN CLASSIC LIBRARY**
is offering some of the best in romance fiction—
great old classics from our early publishing lists.
Complete and mail this coupon today!

FREE BONUS BOOK

Harlequin Reader Service

In U.S.A. P.O. Box 52040
Phoenix, AZ 85072-2040

In Canada 649 Ontario Street
Stratford, Ontario N5A 6W2

Please send me the following novels from the Harlequin Classic Library. I am enclosing my cheque or money order for $1.50 for each novel ordered, plus 75¢ to cover postage and handling. If I order all nine titles at one time, I will receive a FREE book, *Village Doctor*, by Lucy Agnes Hancock.

☐ 136 **Love Is My Reason** (#494)
Mary Burchell

☐ 137 **This Merry Bond** (#583)
Sara Seale

☐ 138 **The Happy Enterprise** (#487)
Eleanor Farnes

☐ 139 **The Primrose Bride** (#988)
Kathryn Blair

☐ 140 **My Heart Has Wings** (#483)
Elizabeth Hoy

☐ 141 **Master of Hearts** (#1047)
Averil Ives

☐ 142 **The Enchanted Trap** (#951)
Kate Starr

☐ 143 **The Garden of Don José** (#928)
Rose Burghley

☐ 144 **Flamingoes on the Lake** (#976)
Isobel Chace

Number of novels checked @ $1.50 each =	$	_____
N.Y. and Ariz. residents add appropriate sales tax	$	_____
Postage and handling	$	.75
	TOTAL $	_____

I enclose _____
(Please send check or money order. We cannot be responsible for cash sent through the mail.)

Prices subject to change without notice.

Name _____
(Please Print)

Address _____
(Apt. no.)

City _____

State/Prov. _____ Zip/Postal Code _____

Offer expires November 30, 1984   CL-116   40556000000

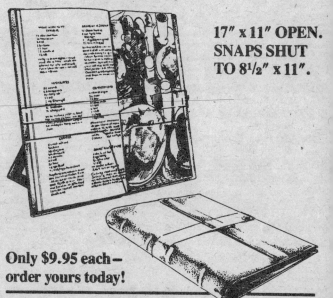